For MS, who's always full of encouragement

And for AJ, who listened

JEWISH SUMMER CAMP MAFIA

MALINA SAVAL

Write Bright Books
Los Angeles

JEWISH SUMMER CAMP MAFIA

7:15 A.M. Reveille

Shalom to Camp Kippewanscot
We're mighty glad you're here
It's Manischewitz Friday nights
Then out to the bar for beer
Rah!
Rah!
We'll send you in
We'll send you in
Hail! Hail! The mighty shot!
Hail! Hail! The gang's all hail
Shalom to Kippewanscot!

— Camp Kippewanscot fight song

Out of all the Jewish summer camps in the country he had to walk into mine.

He couldn't have picked one with a more Jewish-sounding name like Camp Yavneh in New Hampshire or Camp Ramah in the Berkshires or Camp B'nai B'rith in upstate New York. He had to go to the one Reform Jewish sleep-away camp on the entire eastern seaboard with a name that sounded like a Native American casino and an optional (but not required) kosher meal plan. He had to pick the one Reform Jewish sleep-away camp on the entire eastern seaboard where I somehow found myself spending the summer as a reluctant counselor to a bunk of bratty, prematurely full-chested eleven-year-old girls with live-in Panamanian nannies and iPods downloaded with terrible, tweeny Top 40 pop songs.

It was summer, late June, in a mountain town in the Poconos, Pennsylvania. It wasn't even really a town. Just a stretch of farmland and a waxy lake with a tiny island

9

in the middle of it where the camp kept its sailboats, lifejackets and canoes. Swimming lessons were held in a cordoned-off section in which dangling feet skimmed slimy lake grass. There was a gas station and a convenient store that sold cigarettes and scratch tickets and orange and blue-dyed ice cream in little circular paper cups with miniature plastic spoons.

Jewish population in winter: 0

Jewish population in summer: 487

Barrie was the one who told me about Camp Kippewanscot. Barrie—named so because her parents had wanted a boy; her mother had fertility issues back before it was on trend — was my ABFF (Almost Best Friend Forever) from home. We had nothing in common save for a postal code and that for seven years we attended the same three-day-a week (Sun., Tues., Thu.) supplementary Hebrew school.

We met when were six-years-old and bored out of our minds in Mr. Rosov's amazingly lame Jewish Holidays and Customs class. One Sunday, Barrie and I were banished to the rabbi's office for laughing during the scene in which Pharaoh's daughter bathes naked in the Nile during the annual Passover screening of *The Ten Commandments*. As a punishment, we had to write NUDITY IS NOT FUNNY—in Hebrew ("*Irom ze lo divar matzkhik*")—fifty times on the chalkboard, which looking back was actually a really progressive cultural message. It's the first time that I can remember feeling proud of being Jewish.

Back then, Barrie's dad owned six McDonald's across the greater Metropolitan Boston area. Every year he would add a franchise, so that by the time we were sophomores in high school—me at a public one with a rep for sub-par standardized

test scores; she at a Jewish day school where most of the kids spent a year in Israel

getting drunk at a bar in the Russian Compound neighborhood of Jerusalem before

college—Mr. Michelson, proprietor of some twenty golden arches, was dubbed "The

Kosher Burger King" of New England. The moniker landed him in court when that

other international burger chain sued for copyright infringement. Barrie's dad won—

you can't copyright a catchphrase—and with his settlement money he bought up ten

more McDonald's.

Barrie hated him.

"He a total hypocrite," she'd complain, ripping open the plastic baggies stuffed

with vegetarian sandwiches that her mother would pack as a snack when we met up to

hang out over the weekends. "I mean, I live in a house where pork is verboten but my

dad makes his living selling sausage McMuffins to plenty of Jews that don't give a shit

about kosher dietary laws."

Truth was, Barrie didn't care about the ethical ramifications. She just thrilled to

any excuse to be pissed off at her dad. She was a rich kid who spent her entire

childhood scrambling to come up with ways in which her parents had screwed her up.

It was her birthright.

"Fuck them!" she would declare, seemingly at random and about nothing in

particular.

There was a string of Saturdays the spring of sophomore year when, as an act of

rebellion, Barrie would invite me over on Shabbat afternoons to commit as many halakhic transgressions as humanly possible. Halakhah is the Hebrew word for Jewish law—why we don't work on Saturdays, how many days we celebrate Passover, the reason that we don't eat cheeseburgers or anything with mayonnaise (actually, this is more custom than law). Barrie wanted to break all the rules. And she wanted me as her (not so kosher) partner in crime. So we'd sit cross-legged on her queen-sized bed while reading stolen copies of her mother's dirty romance novels from the 80's (*Wifey* by Judy Blume was a favorite for all the sex scenes), log onto porn sites on her pink MacBook, and stuff our faces with contraband Happy Meals and Big Macs that we'd sneaked into the house, mischievously spreading crumbs all over her lavender Ralph Lauren bedspread.

"I'm your adventure," Barrie liked to say, a mischievous glint in her hazel eyes. "And you are my reality check." What we each wanted out of life was different, but we both wanted things. And *badly*. And *now*. For Barrie, that meant a hot boy with a fast car to French kiss. For me, that meant getting perfect grades, early acceptance to an Ivy League school—preferably Yale for its English department and because Claire Danes went there— and becoming a famous newspaper journalist. And so our friendship blossomed.

Barrie had never been to Camp Kippewanscot, but a bunch of the so-called "cool" kids from her basic-level Topics in Bereshit class (aka "Baby Bible") had gone every summer. "It was awesome," they gushed to Barrie during end-of-semester study groups revolving around six-packs of Red Bull and debates on whether or not Adam and Eve ever actually did it. Per Barrie, a resounding *Yes!*

"I mean, hello," she'd say, "you're a girl stuck all alone with a guy in some garden running around naked. All that dust to dust and rib and snake and apple crap. Give me a break. They obviously *fucked*."

Spring semester, senior year, and Barrie had no pressing summer plans. For the past two seasons she'd spent July and August on Nantucket with her mom. Mrs. Michaelson had divorced Barrie's father after she discovered that he was having an affair with the 21 year-old Puerto Rican McD's manager of the Randolph, Massachusetts location. In a way, Barrie was relieved. Now she finally had an actual real reason to hate her father. It was like everything she ever wanted came true.

"My dad is such an asshole!" she exclaimed when the news first hit, beaming with devilish excitement. "All those years he barred bacon from the house? When he's nothing but a pig that's been screwing some skanky Catholic chick? Who bleaches her mustache with Jolène and wears a nose ring that she got from a cart in the Braintree mall?" Oh, how she laughed and laughed.

Her father's infidelity made Barrie furious at her mother as well. Obviously, she believed it was partly her fault. "If she stopped eating donuts and spending half her life shopping and going to therapy four times a week and complaining to her girlfriends on the phone about how she and my dad never have *sex*." She'd ramble on and on over the iPhone that she'd scored as a bribe following her parents' split. "Maybe if she *exercised* once in a while then maybe my dad wouldn't have cheated on her."

"Barrie," I told her, "You're mom has nothing to do with this. That's sort of the point. He obviously wasn't thinking of her at all—"

"Let's get out of here for the summer," she cut in. "I'm so sick of my mom and all those bitchy, bitter women in her divorce support group with their beige Talbots shorts and their stupid nautical canvas beach bags from L.L. Bean with their maiden names monogrammed in huge capitals letters. Like, their names are *so* important. Like, 'OK, I'm divorced! And I'm back to my old name! Before I met my asshole husband!'" Barrie sighed. "And I can't deal with summer school even if graduating depends upon finally passing Introduction to Midrash. Fucking useless. All those rabbis sitting around on their fat asses arguing about the Torah? Didn't anybody have *jobs* back then? Like, seriously, when is Rashi's commentary on the book of Genesis ever going to come up in regular conversation? When will I possibly ever need to know about Rashi[1]?"

"Well, you will in order to graduate, " I reminded her.

But Barrie never listened to anything I said. This was probably the reason that we managed to get along so well. So obsessed with herself, she had no idea that she never made sense about almost anything. And I never really took anything that she said all that seriously, so it all kind of worked out. We hadn't had a fight in ten years.

"I've got an idea," she announced with a flourish in her voice and a silent, stream-of-consciousness drum roll in her head: "Camp."

It took a moment to process. "*Camp?*"

---

[1] Otherwise known as Rabbi Shlomo Yitzhaki, medieval French Rabbi about whom Barrie knows nothing.

"I've never been to overnight camp and I think it will be a really good experience. Everybody who's ever been to camp tells me that the counselors have way more fun than the campers. It's all about late night make-out sessions, smoking pot, getting into trashy bars in hick towns with fake I.D.s. We would have such an awesome time."

"But we don't smoke pot," I said.

"So? We'll start! We're way behind on that anyway. I mean, how are we going to survive socially in college if we don't know how to smoke weed? I don't want to be one of those annoying freshman that coughs up a joint at a keg party."

A few months back Barrie was convinced that her mother was dealing weed. She called in an absolute state after eavesdropping on her mother telling a friend that she'd signed up to volunteer with the American Jewish Joint Distribution Committee. She had no idea that her mother was raising funds for Haiti and not hash.

"We don't have to go to camp to get stoned," I told Barrie. "I mean, if that's your primary goal."

"My primary goal is to get out of here," she huffed. "And I hear the guys at Camp Kippewanscot are super gorgeous. We're practically guaranteed to meet a hot Jewish guy."

I hesitated. "I don't know," I told her. "I'm supposed to go to California to visit Berkowitz."

Matthew Berkowitz was my BGF (Best Guy Friend) in the entire world. We'd met on an organized El Al Airlines trip to Israel the year prior when we were both sixteen and traveling with our families. He was from Los Angeles and slept with girls

that had long swingy ponytails and wore miniskirts from Kitson. And I was a virgin

who still entertained romantic notions about love and wore khaki shorts from The

Gap. We were both really embarrassed that our parents followed us everywhere and

lost them in the crowd every chance we got.

During our six-week chaperoned romp around the country, I fell madly in love

with Matthew's best friend Ben.

Benjamin Katz was a child actor who'd had a guest-starring role on *Zoey 101*

and felt me up for the first time on a narrow bunk bed with scratchy bedding in a

kibbutz (it's like a farm but everyone wears sandals) on the Sea of Galilee. Ben had icy

blue eyes and light brown hair and was taller than any of the Jewish boys I knew from

back home. I recognized him immediately from a bit part he'd played on *Gossip Girl*

(Barrie had made me watch it). "You were really good," I told him, even though it was

a non-speaking part. He replied that it was "method acting" and did I want to see his

headshot?

The first time Ben and I kissed was on the beach in Tel Aviv under a shooting

star, which would be corny if it weren't true (Ok fine, it still is corny). But he was also a

self-absorbed actor who had a hard time relating to anyone who didn't want to talk

about his upcoming role as Student #4 in an episode of *One Tree Hill*. He kept

practicing his one line—"I'll meet you after class, OK?"—throughout our tour of

Jerusalem's Old City. During our day trip to the Banyas, a lush forested area with

postcard-perfect waterfalls, he asked me to snap pictures of him in front of every palm tree. He did Batman imitations on our sunrise hike up Masada, as I panted and puffed

struggling to keep up with him, dropping my water bottle and asthma inhaler

somewhere between the remains of Herod's bathhouse and the Roman Ramp (Every

Jewish kid I knew had asthma, even if we didn't. We all had the same allergist and

Ventolin was the most coveted drug, easier to get than Ritalin and way cooler than

Whip-Its). During a music class one Shabbat afternoon, I tried desperately to impress

Ben with my newly acquired shofar blowing abilities. But he grabbed the shofar and

stuck it in his shorts and pretended it was a giant penis. And I thought he was so cool.

I know, it sounds pathetic. But it was just a few years back that I was twelve and

really, really, *really* ugly (really). I was at my first United Synagogue Youth social mixer

and not a single boy asked me to dance. I had a mullet cut with a little tail in the back

and these big white buckteeth and my breath smelled like a retainer. And I was wearing

these horrible striped trousers that my grandmother had bought for me on a recent

trip to Brazil not realizing they were meant for a boy. I essentially looked like a Jonas

brother as I sat on the edge of the bima (a stage in a synagogue sanctuary) listening to a

Katy Perry song and hoping beyond hope that somebody would ask me to dance.

Somebody did actually—a girl. Who thought that I was a hot boy who looked just like

a Jonas brother. All of the girl's friends thought that I was a boy, too, because they

kept giggling and pushing her towards me. That I was a hot boy all the girls wanted to

dance with was little consolation for the fact that I was actually an ugly girl who

wanted to dance with a boy.

So you can imagine my excitement when I met Ben that a boy finally liked me enough to ignore me.

That same summer Matthew dated this slutty French-Jewish girl named Amélie who wore a string bikini in the Dead Sea when the rest of us wore one pieces, didn't shave our legs for a week and prayed to God we didn't get our periods (The world's highest concentration of mineral salt + menstrual flow = worst fucking burning pain in the entire female universe).

One day, late at night, walking from my kibbutz bunk to the communal bathroom, I caught Matthew and Amélie doing it in the banana fields. I heard desperate moans and the squish of bananas as they rubbed around on top of one another. I felt a stab of hot jealousy and I couldn't really figure out why.

Sophomore year, when I flew to California over Columbus Day weekend to tour UCLA as a ruse to see Ben Katz and lose my virginity to him, Ben was predictably a total asshole. We did it with my socks still on and a Feist video on MTV. He sent me back to my hotel in a cab. Which I paid for with the spending money I'd saved up babysitting the ADHD kid down the street. Who used to snort his Ritalin through a straw and never shared.

After that, Berkowitz and I were the ones to keep in touch. We exchanged daily emails and had marathon text message sessions. We were both major movie buffs and spent hours reciting our favorite lines from classic flicks like *Hannah and Her Sisters*: "How the hell do I know why there were Nazis? I don't know how the can opener works!" We called one another by our last names just like Robert Redford and Barbra Streisand in *The Way We Were*: "Oh, Berkowitz! Oh, Mendelssohn!" And we decided that someday when we were done dating loser boys that stuck shofars down their shorts and French sluts that slid around on bananas, that we would definitely get married to one another.

"Can't you go visit Berkowitz and *then* go to camp?" asked Barrie after I'd told her all of this. "You're not even officially dating the guy. You're not visiting him the *whole* summer, right?"

"No," I told her. "But I don't have a fake I.D. anyway. How am I going to sneak into bars? And where are we going to get pot?"

"Come on," she begged. "*Please.* I can't bear to spend the summer here and I've got no one else to go with me. It'll be so much fun."

I tried to picture it. "I don't know, Barrie," I said. "I've gone to summer camp as a camper. You don't know what these Jewish camps are like. They're like the Mafia. The head counselors are like Tony Soprano and the campers are like Meadow and unless you've gone there your whole life as a camper you're totally ostracized. Worse, you're targeted as someone to make fun of, to humiliate. It's impossible to finagle your way into the popular crowd. And if your parents are stupid enough to follow the packing list and send you away with 4 t-shirts, 1 pair of sneakers, 1 pair of water shoes and a pair of blue shorts and a white polo shirt for Shabbat – you might as well wear a sign that says LOSER on your forehead. It's pretty hardcore. Campers go where their parents went, their parents went where *their* parents went, and *their* parents went where their parents went. All the way back to Ellis Island. All the way back to the Pale of Settlement. All the way back to Mesopotamia. All the way back to Camp Garden of

Eden where Cain and Abel were head counselors. Being a counselor at a summer camp where you've never been a camper is like committing social suicide. It's like asking to be whacked and your head stuffed in a bowling ball bag and dumped at sea. Trust me. We'll never fit in."

I thought about all the long, hot summers that I'd spent as a kid at Camp Ruach, an all-girls non-denominational Jewish summer camp in upstate New York. The name meant spirit, but unless you'd been going since you were six years old, the other girls treated you like you were soap scum in the shower. You never got the electives you wanted, you wound up in the remedial swimming group even if you passed the disrobing safety test, and you were excluded from all the super cool secret camp clubs with secret languages and specific trendy clothing requirements. And you didn't have a hope in hell of making out with any of the hot kitchen boys from Kentucky who paraded around shirtless and smoked Merits on their nights off. You were lucky if you got to swap spit with the skinny, nerdy boys with big glasses from the Jewish boys camp across the lake.

Things weren't any easier on the other side of Lake Buttermilk Falls. My little brother Bucky—Bernard, but since the botched orthodontics job a few years back when he was ten and accidentally given the wrong sized retainer, nobody ever called him that—spent summers at Camp Simcha getting his head dunked in the toilet by one camper while another camper flushed. And this was because he was popular and had been going every summer since he was seven. If you weren't popular, nobody dunked your head anywhere—you were just ignored. And that was the worst kind of unpopular.

For the three years we were both away at camp at the same time, we saw one another on visiting day when our parents treated us to Friday's. The summer he was nine he bounded across camp toward the car with his hair all soaking wet shouting, "I got a swirly! Mom, Dad, I got a swirly!" He wouldn't shut up about it. He thought he was the coolest person on the planet.

But Barrie didn't quite get it. "What are you saying?" she asked. "That you want a swirly?"

"No, I don't want a swirly—"

"Look," she scoffed. "I'm not exactly unpopular here at school. OK? I'm not worried about not fitting in. And if you're with me, everyone will love you. People love me, Mushky. They'll love you, too."

My real name is Mushka. But everyone calls me Mushky. My dad started the trend, partly I think because he felt a little bad about burdening me with such a mouthful of a name: Mushka Malka Mendelssohn. It's Yiddish[2]: Mushka means *spice*, Malka means *queen*, Mendelssohn translates as something like *Son of the comforter* (I looked it up on one of those Jewish name Web sites) and I'm pretty sure nobody in my entire extended family knows what it means.

As unfortunate as it might seem, I like my name. I like that my parents gave me a name that's so decidedly Jewish even if the rest of us weren't. I like that my mom

---

[2] A combo-language of German and Hebrew spoken by Eastern European Jews

won't think twice about racing out to Marshalls on a Saturday morning if the urge

strikes to buy discounted dishtowels, but at the same time insisted that my classic rock-

themed DJ disco bat mitzvah party at the Courtyard Marriot started after sundown

when Shabbat ended because, "Jews don't play music on the Shabbos." (I did not like

that she hired a blind, Jewish accordion player to serenade out-of-town guests with

tunes from the *Fiddler on the Roof* soundtrack at the Sunday morning brunch).

In any case, it was a double standard that I could live with because, frankly, it's

hard for my mother to resist a sale, but how hard is it to plan a one-time party for a

Saturday night? We were Jewish where it mattered. And names matter the most.

Mushky is a dead giveaway. There's no way that I could ever hide from it or pretend to

be anything that I'm not. It actually makes my life less complicated in some strange

way.

"Summer camp is different," I warned Barrie. "Trust me. I would have gone

back to my own camp to be a counselor but I skipped the summer they picked C.I.T's

when I was fourteen and did that Wellesley College gifted and talented summer

program and—"

"Mushky, you're crazy," she said, impatience rising in her voice. "It's going to

be fun. I already know this one guy going. His name is Ron and he's totally hot. He

wears a yarmulke outside of school but he's sexy. He's into poetry and he doesn't have

a unibrow like some of those other religious guys. He was the T.A. in my algebra class

last year and he already got in early to Brown. I hear he's majoring in Intellectual

History, or one of those girly majors where the guys are good kissers. You'd for *sure* like him."

"Barrie," I pointed out. "You never go to your algebra class."

"That's not true," she countered. "I clock in for attendance."

"I don't know, Barrie. I was thinking it might be a good idea for me to take a summer class or look for an internship or something. You know, pad my college applications with a little something extra. Getting into Yale is going to be pretty cut throat, especially with it being such a huge draw among young movie stars. We've got to start thinking about college."

It was a dumb thing to say to a girl who most likely, no matter what her ideological objections, would eventually go to work for her dad as an international ambassador for the Super Value Meal.

"Mushky, we're going to be *seniors*. We've got one more year of high school before real life begins. Why would you possibly waste that time worrying about what comes after? This could be the last summer before life gets *serious*."

Barrie did have a point. Once in a blue moon she did. It could be the last summer that summer would be spoken of as such, a division of time, a clear seasonal distinction between Work and Fun. The last summer we would even have a summer of which to speak. The next summer I'd slave away at the local Barnes & Noble saving money for college. Summer after, I'd take a respectable but underpaid on-campus job assisting an English professor. After that, I'd take my junior year abroad in Israel, interning as a baby journalism rat for a local rag, reporting on pita vendors arrested on charges of noise pollution and Israeli astronauts that kept kosher in outer space, and in my spare time researching my senior thesis on *Anti-Semitism in Modern American Ethnic Literature.* Classes at Hebrew University would extend from October through mid-August of the next year. I'd return to school for senior year where I would take a full course load, complete my senior thesis, suffer a series of minor nervous breakdowns when my computer crashed and erased my thesis and I had to completely rewrite it from memory (and use my asthma inhaler for real). I'd graduate *summa cum laude,* land another respectable job as an assistant to a newspaper editor in New York City. I'd work summer after summer after *summer…*

Barrie was right. After this summer, summer would no longer be.

"OK," I consented. "Let's go."

But just as I'd made my decision to go to camp, turned down an attractive offer from a divorced, alcoholic lesbian English professor at Boston University to be her summer research bitch on a book that she was writing about drunks in modern American literature, and sent in my application form and received my personalized acceptance call from the Camp Kippewanscot director himself, Barrie's dad dialed her up and invited her to spend the summer on a beach resort in Thailand, where he was overseeing the grand re-opening of a McDonald's.

"You hate your dad," I told her.

"It's *Thailand,*" she said. "All of the McDonalds were destroyed in the Tsunami. It's my duty to give back."

It was a ridiculous argument, but I did the research before calling her out. According to the Internet, there were 104 McDonalds in Thailand, and yes, one was in Phuket, where the heart of the Tsunami struck. The chain's telephone number was listed. I thought about calling to check in on its restoration efforts because even though the tsunami happened six years ago, some structures were still in shambles. I had no idea if rebuilding the McD's was a huge priority over there or not. But then I remembered how furious my father got when I phoned my third cousin Tova in Toronto and talked for 45 minutes during a peak hour, and that was still in North America. He'd flip if I dialed Southeast Asia.

I was screwed.

Barrie decided to bail.

I was going to camp alone.

My parents kept telling me how good it would be for me. "Maybe you'll meet someone," they both kept saying, which is hands down THE most annoying thing a Jewish parent can ever tell his or her child. Because it was never as encouraging as they tried to make it sound. It was never about meeting someone who was going to slip you the answers to the AP Biology exam, or about meeting someone that might ghost write your college admissions essay so that you wouldn't have to bother: "How would you describe yourself as a human being in 800 words or less?" It was never about meeting someone that could score you backstage passes the next time Rufus Wainwright played the Wang Center. It was never about anything good. It was always about meeting a boy.

A Jewish boy.

I didn't resent my parents the way Barrie did. For starters, neither had ever cheated on one another. And while my family was flexible when it came to Jewish dietary customs, I would never say hypocritical. We were, as my father quipped, "Kosher convenient." No pork or shellfish allowed in the house. Ever. (And if you're really interested, and really bored, you can read the book of Leviticus to find out why. And duh, there are no shellfish in the desert!). But once in a great while we'd dine out at Chinese restaurants, and only on Christmas day or Sunday nights when the rest of our synagogue congregation was committing culinary transgressions as well. And we never ordered the lobster (too red, too treyf[3], too many claws). But for catered affairs like bar and bat mitzvahs and weddings, my parents insisted that it had to come from Provender Kosher Catering. This suited me just fine because, frankly, I have a difficult time eating anything that screams while being boiled. Bottom line, my parents pretty much let me eat whatever I wanted.

As for them caring whom I dated? Well, that was an entirely different story.

---

[3] So not kosher they wouldn't even serve it in a "kosher style" Jewish deli

7:45 A.M. Flag Raising

I never meant to fall in love with Devin McGillicudy. Then again, no one ever

means to fall in love with anybody. But when I met Devin, love was seriously the last

thing on my mind.

Which is inevitably why it happened.

Love is like losing a set of car keys—if I had a car, but I don't; I take the T

everywhere—that you keep looking for under the couch. Six months later, you find

them in the empty ice tray in the freezer compartment of the refrigerator while you're

searching for an ice cream sandwich to eat during MTV's *Sixteen and Pregnant*.

It was my first day at camp, and I wasn't sure what I was looking for as I exited

the Newark International Airport other than a bus with a blinking sign on its

windshield that said CAMP KIPPEWANSCOT that embarrassed me to the point of

wearing fake Ray Ban sunglasses from Forever 21 as I boarded it. I was seventeen years

old and an incoming senior in high school and I was getting on a school bus to

summer camp.

I wanted to kill Barrie. I knew absolutely no one.

I had no idea why I had come, no idea how I'd possibly been coerced into such

a compromising position, no idea why I hadn't backed out when Barrie did. I could

have done something practical like take a 20-credit course load of summer classes and

graduate from high school a semester early. Or something impractical like volunteer with Habitat For Humanity and sing Jesus Loves Us songs while rebuilding a school destroyed in the ninth ward during Hurricane Katrina. Anything that made more sense than spending eight weeks of my Last Summer in the middle of a muggy, bug-infested, rurally situated, co-ed Reform Jewish camp with optional Saturday morning Shabbat services and watered-down Manischewitz.

Maybe I was too responsible. They had offered me a job and I took it. Maybe I was afraid of letting people down. *Yale doesn't accept quitters!* Or at least that's what I kept telling myself.

As I slogged toward the large rec hall where our first staff meeting was being held, I looked for the hot Jewish guy that Barrie had promised.

"Ron?" I asked a few random guys with wavy hair and thin eyebrows. "Ron?"

I looked everywhere, behind every tree and tennis court and archery range and art shack and bunk that I passed.

I didn't see him.

I pictured him waiting for me on the docks by the lake, head of windsurf, with thick, windswept hair and a faded maroon Harvard T-shirt, with excellent job prospects for when he graduated. He'd have really sophisticated/borderline snobbish indie taste in music and listen to NPR and teach me everything about the new Sufjan Stevens and Guided by Voices albums. He'd be tall and beautiful and like me right away.

He was nowhere.

My guess was he'd backed out, too. Or else he'd never existed and Barrie made the whole thing up just to get me to go with her to camp. The sticky June heat was giving me a headache behind my eyes and I was starting to get that sinking feeling in my stomach that comes when you know that you've made a really bad decision and there's no way of getting out of it.

I was stuck. I was never getting out. There was not a hot Jewish guy in sight.

Not that I didn't think Jewish guys were hot. Ben Katz was hot. And Shia LaBeouf. Paul Rudd. Berkowitz, of course. Beck (even though he was a practicing Scientologist). Jake Gyllenhaal. Joaquin Phoenix (he's Jewish, seriously). And then all the graying, half-Jewish guys like Sean Penn who were even hotter than the full-on Jews. And the quarter-Jewish guys like Harrison Ford who probably didn't even know they had any Jewish genes in them until Adam Sandler sang a song about them. Adam Sandler. Jon Stewart. Dr. Drew Pinsky was kind of hot if you're into that helping-people-get-off-drugs-while-becoming-a-celebrity-yourself thing. Bruce Springsteen (OK, so he's not Jewish, but he's Jew-*ish*). Steven Spielberg (thirty years ago).

I would have dated any one of them. Because I'm not the spiteful self-hating type who dismisses the possibility of hooking up with someone Jewish or short or ugly or all three just so I can destroy the last flickering hope of my Russian-Jewish grandparents to finally add a bone cancer specialist (or at the very least a pediatrician) to the family. But, it didn't matter, because none of those guys went to Camp Kippewanscot. One glance around, and it was clear that I'd suffered the tragic misfortune of landing at a Jewish summer camp where, if the counselors weren't girls, then they certainly weren't good looking and if they happened to be good looking, well,

then they certainly weren't Jewish.

How could I tell? Easy. I can sniff out a Jewish guy from miles away. It's not the

way he looks, not exactly. It's more ineffable than all that, it's an energy, a

nonchalance, an air of bravado that in Jewish guys is almost always lacking.

And sometimes it's the hair.

I'd seen that kind of hair only once before, on a family vacation to San Diego,

California when I was ten. He was riding a wave in the foamy ocean, his body all

bronzed and glistening. It was the color of pale straw baking in the sun, shiny and

incandescent to the point where you could almost see your reflection in it.

"Hi," said the voice behind hair. "I'm Devin. But you can call me Dev."

And then there's the name. And from thereon in it's hopelessly undeniable.

There is not a Jewish guy on the planet named Devin But You Can Call Me Dev. Not

even among the most secular unaffiliated of Jews. Not even in North Dakota. Not even

in Wyoming. Red state Jews with the name Devin do. Not. Exist.

"Hi," I said. "I'm..." For the first time in my entire life I hesitated when I said it.

Guilt the size of a matzoh ball got lodged in the back of my throat. Finally, I got it out:

"Mushky."

He smiled, a white flash of curiosity. I was a traitor. I was desecrating the

collective memory of the entire Jewish people. Three thousand years of history and it

was all ending, right here, right now, ten minutes before a Reform Jewish summer

camp staff meeting. Suddenly, all I could see was the twisted up face of my dead

Russian-Jewish great-grandmother, her black eyes glaring at me with fiery contempt, her mouth undulating in menacing slow-motion like an animated monster in a Disney Pixar flick, warning me to back away from this beautiful, blond Gentile lest I destroy any and every chance of the Jewish people to go forth and multiply. My great-grandmother was born in a shtetl (Yiddish name for a little town) and grew up in a family of thirteen children and twice as many cows. She survived the Holocaust by hiding for two years in an abandoned barn in Galicia, Poland. And she came to America with nothing but five dollars and an apple in her pocket to create a better life for her family. All so that I could throw it all away on a guy who looked like he popped straight off the pages of *Surfer* Magazine.

So I said my name again. I enunciated it loud and clear so there was absolutely no mistaking it: "Mushky." Pause. "Mendelssohn."

Dev smiled again. "I heard you the first time." He looked me up and down, narrowing his impossibly big eyes, glistening pools of shaygetz[4] baby blue. "Very cool name."

I could tell that he liked me. Liked my name, liked my khaki shorts and dark fake Ray Bans that I had yet to take off because I was still so embarrassed to be here. I slid them off so he could see my eyes, rims of dark Black Sea brown.

In front of us, spread out on the field, were hundreds of campers' trunks sealed with thick bands of UPS duct tape. Dev walked toward them and motioned for me to follow. I lagged a few paces behind and watched the way his legs moved. He sauntered

---

[4] Hot non-Jewish guy with blond hair

more than walked, gait vertical, shoulders back. His hips swayed a little, arms held evenly at each side. He strode confidently across the grass, moving in an almost rhythmic motion, his thigh muscles lean and tight.

"Are you an athlete?" I asked.

Dev found a black leather trunk and sat down upon it. "No," he said. "Do I look like one?"

I shrugged. "Maybe," I said.

He patted the empty spot beside him. "Sit down."

There wasn't much room, but I sat. I felt the heat from his torso through his t-shirt against my side. My heart thumped. A few beads of sweat collected in the crevice of my B-cup cleavage.

"So why are you here?" he asked.

Eyes squinting, I surveyed the pell-mell arrangement of trunks, duffle bags and boxes. I shook my head. "I don't know," I answered.

"Well," he said, "you must know a little."

"A friend was going to come. She backed out."

"That's too bad."

"Yea," I said. "I know."

"Too bad for her."

"Yea, well, she's in Thailand rebuilding a McDonald's."

He laughed. "No," I said. "I'm serious."

"You could have backed out, too."

"I know," I sighed. "I'm just realizing that now."

He stretched his arms high above his head and pushed his feet against the grass and tilted his head back so that his face was bathed in sunlight. I studied his expression, his mouth, and his slightly parted lips. I got a closer look at his mouth, his gap-toothed smile. He had a small chip on his front left tooth, which no Jewish boy would ever have because his Jewish mother would have made sure that he got it capped. Even if it meant she had to sell her kidney to afford the dentist bill.

"What about you?" I asked. "Why are you here?"

"Oh, you know," he yawned. "I'm in college."

"And?"

"And, I have no idea what I'm going to do when I get out."

"So you came *here*?"

He turned and looked at me. "What's your specialty?" he asked.

"In what?"

"Here. They signed you up to teach something, right?"

"Oh," I said. "Yea." I fumbled around in my back pocket for the folded slip of paper they'd sent me in the mail. I smoothed it out and handed it to him.

"Radio broadcasting?" he said, his brow crinkling. "What do you know about radios?"

"I don't," I told him. "I have no idea why they signed me up for that. I suppose gymnastics was already taken?"

"You don't know anything about radios?"

"I listen to the radio, and I love music, but yea, I don't know a single thing about teaching a radio broadcasting class. I don't even own a radio aside of the one in my parents' car. They still don't have Sirius. And they hardly ever let me drive it anyway."

"Does anybody own a radio anymore?" Dev asked.

"I don't think so."

"So it's a completely pointless specialty."

"I guess—"

"Antiquated."

"Well, I didn't pick—"

"So you don't really need to be here." He cocked his head to the side and with it strands of pale yellow fell softly across his forehead.

"Ok," I said, "and what do you do that's so relevant? Head of archery? Head of kite surfing—"

"Computers."

"Computers?"

"Computers," he repeated. "And unlike you, I actually do know something about it."

I scrunched up my nose. I was having a difficult time picturing a guy that looked like he leapt out of a Swedish shampoo commercial downloading Internet software and reconfiguring JPEG files. I wanted him to be doing something a bit...sexier. Like lifeguarding. Or head of tennis. Or sailing instructor.

"Do you major in computer science or something?" I asked.

"God, no," he said, flinching like I'd offended him. "Computer *graphics*. Fine Arts. Double major. You know, painting, sketching, drawing—"

"So, shouldn't you be, you know, head of arts and crafts?"

"The computer shack is air conditioned. The arts and crafts shack isn't."

"Makes sense," I nodded. "So where do you go to school?"

"Emerson," he said. "Do you know it?"

My heart did a backwards flip. If my heart were a Chinese gymnast, it would have stuck the landing and scored a perfect ten. Emerson wasn't Harvard, but it was five stops away on the green line if you got on the red line and then transferred at Park Street.

"No way," I said in my best casual cool. "I'm from Boston. I live really close to Emerson."

"That's crazy," he said. "I've got my own apartment right on Commonwealth Ave."

Own. Apartment. Commonwealth Ave.

"Cool," I said. "And you're an *artist*."

"I am," he sighed. "Maybe I'll get into computer animation. Or advertising. Or MTV videos. Or work the night shift at the 7-Eleven."

Maybe it was the way my mouth fell slack on the words 7 and Eleven that Dev made an extra point of smiling. "Don't worry," he assured, resting his hand upon my leg. "I've got one more year of college. I'm sure I'll graduate and get a job."

"I never said you wouldn't."

He drew away his hand, right as I was hoping he'd move it upward toward my thigh. He looked at my eyes, my hair, my ears, and drew his hand across my cheek. "You know," he said, "I could paint you."

Four sexiest words a Gentile had ever said to me.

"Yea," I said. "That would be pretty cool."

He looked at his watch. "I think it's about time for our staff meeting," he said.

He stood up from the camper's trunk, tossing back his ridiculously toss-able blonde, blonde hair. "Let's go," he said, and motioned me along.

"How old are you?" I asked, trailing behind. He was strong and broad and his arms were big enough to get lost inside of them for days.

"Twenty," he said. "Twenty-one in August." He paused. "And you?"

I thought about it for a moment longer than I should have. "Eighteen."

"Yea," he said, like he didn't quite believe me.

I sort of tossed back my shoulder-length brown hair even though it wasn't as pretty as his. "I'm an incoming senior," I told him. "Actually, I'm seventeen."

"So why did you lie?"

"I don't know," I shrugged. "My birthday's in January and everybody else's seems earlier because I'm young for my grade. I actually missed the cutoff to start kindergarten. When I was four-and-a-half they were going to stick me in some transitional kindergarten program with all the kids with receptive and expressive speech disorders and make me take a short yellow bus to school. But my mom refused and let me stay home for the year and watch *Sesame Street* and *Days of Our Lives* and there was this huge fight with the school board and anyway, I never even ended up going to kindergarten. Went straight to first grade."

"So you're advanced," he said. He patted me on the back. "Which is a good thing."

We waited around as a throng of counselors collected by the front door of the rec hall. Dev kept looking at me and I shifted around nervously, looking for a cross or an Italian horn or something sparkly and tacky around his neck.

"What are you looking at?" he asked.

"Nothing," I answered. "What's your last name?"

"McGillicudy."

It was as I suspected. I should have run away right there and then. Sprinted. Made a mad dash. Sprouted wings and flown. "McGilli—*what*?"

"Like Mushky *Mendelssohn* is any better?"

"It's a lot better. It's alliterative."

Dev raised a brow like he had no idea what the word meant, which worried me. "I'm Irish," he said. "Very Irish. Irish *Catholic*."

He peered at the dainty, diamond *chai* around my neck (symbol meaning "life" in Hebrew), a bat mitzvah gift from my rich cousins in Scarsdale. I'd been wearing it for four years straight. Non-Jews would come up to me all the time asking if it was an elephant. It was too big of a pain to explain that it wasn't, so I'd just tell them that it was. Sometimes, for fun, I would tell them that it was a camel.

"Pretty necklace," he said.

"Thanks," I said, "It's a—"

"I know what it is," Dev said. He pulled out a long, silvery chain from underneath his T-shirt. "I've gone my own symbolic charm."

It was worse than a cross.

It was a *Claddaugh*.

8:00 A.M. Breakfast

"Morning, Sunshine."

Dev sat across from me at the breakfast table, smirking periodically. On the table was a spread of institution food offerings: ceramic decanters of lukewarm milk, bowls of generic bran and sugared cereals, blue-ish-white hardboiled eggs, Granny Smith apples and bruised bananas, and baskets of bread and half-toasted toast. When it came time for the blessing before the meal, Dev didn't know any of it:

> We give thanks to God for bread
> Our voices join in happy chorus
> As our prayers are humbly said:
> Baruch atah adonai
> Eloheinu melech ha-olam
> Hamotzi lechem min ha-aretz.
> Aaaaaaamen!

He tried to follow along and mouth the words, but he could never catch up, and he wound up looking like an actor in a badly dubbed Chinese kung-fu movie whose audio is on a two-second delay. But I admired his attempt. It was cute and charming and he was obviously trying to impress me. What semi-pretty Jewish girl doesn't want that in a smoking hot Irish Catholic boy? I watched his lips as they opened and closed and, for a moment, dreamt that he was pulling me slowly toward his ripe parted mouth. Jewish or not Jewish, Dev was the hottest boy I'd ever seen.

"Morning," he said again, because I didn't respond the first time.

"Morning," I yawned, pretending I didn't care. Also, I was totally exhausted. It was staff week and the campers had yet to arrive. It was just the counselors and we ruled the camp. We sat around in circles on the grass late at night, all night, doused in bug spray, smoking cigarettes (I didn't smoke, but held one just to look cool), talking about life back home and what it was that brought each of us to camp. Everyone crafted these phony excuses for not having a REAL job, and some were quite creative. Others, downright creepy. Darren, boys camp head counselor, oozed excitement over being here for his thirteenth summer in a row ("My bat mitzvah year! I get a special camp coffee mug and a hooded sweatshirt!"). His face was kind of squished and he had a nose like Shrek, but he had really sweet and kind eyes. He was forty years old and single. During the regular year he worked at a post-production editing house in Los Angeles, but his job requirements seemed nebulous. "I drive around a lot," he said. "And what's really great is that I get the entire summer off to do what I truly love— working with small children."

Every so often, the camp owner, Uncle Stan, would stroll past on his way to the dining hall or his bunk, patting us on the back for doing a great job sitting around doing nothing. Uncle Stan was a little bit out of it, which is a good thing when it comes to camp owners. He was as portly as a meatball, bald, and spent the bulk of each day either lolling through the dining hall on his cane or rolling across camp in his golf cart. He could never remember anyone's name but was always waving and smiling at everyone, too old and tired to really care about camp anymore.

Uncle Stan's nephew, Uncle Gary, played acting camp director. Uncle Gary—or UG as everyone called him, and his presence truly did elicit that sound— was perhaps the least avuncular person that had ever roamed the planet. He had a deep groove down the middle of his forehead, likely from wearing a permanent glower on his face. Despite his recent lap band surgery, he was still morbidly obese. He was so fat that the airlines made him buy two airplane seats whenever he flew, or at least that's what everyone said. He had beady black eyes and wore thick, horn-rimmed glasses and his nose had a bunch of blackheads on it. He ambled around camp brandishing a giant bullhorn, barking at counselors to stop doing all the things that, so far, made camp fun.

This particular morning, UG was snapping at some female Swedish counselor that was gyrating on the breakfast table doing a pretend striptease. "Get down!" he yelled at the girl. Her name was Elsa Larsson and she was as willowy and lovely as her name implies, with legs as long as sunflower stems, hair a waist-length curtain of strawberry blonde. "Or I'll send you home on the first flight back to Stockholm!"

There was a whole table of Swedish counselors. They looked like Vikings and were all infinitely more beautiful than anyone else at camp. They were all super skinny and super tall, their skin as creamy as a bar of Ivory soap. The Swedes had come for the summer to make enough money for university in Stockholm, which, given the camp salary, was obviously dirt-cheap. At Camp Ruach each season there was a noticeable staff void where once a graduating class of Jewish counselors had been. The Jewish counselors had now gone off to get regular, decent paying summer jobs, typically in either finance or law, though some of them secured non-paying intern positions in medical labs that would help them get into Harvard. The camp was now forced to dip into the international non-Jew talent pool. One summer we had a counselor from

Djibouti, which made him instantly popular. By the middle of August, everybody

wanted to be from Djibouti, even if they couldn't find it on a map.

Camp Kippewanscot had a table of Swedes on one side of the dining hall and

British imports on the other. The Swedes taught ceramics and jewelry making; the

Brits, soccer and copper. The Brits weren't all that much to look at—most of them had

bad teeth from lack of proper dental care—but the Swedes, well, they were even

prettier than Dev. I'm sure it wasn't their intention, but with their voluminous hair and

rosy-cheeked complexions, you could tell the Swedes made all the short, prematurely

balding Jewish staff members feel like primordial dwarfs.

"Get down," UG again demanded of Elsa, the Swedish Striptease.

Elsa whimsically laughed. She lifted up her miniskirt and twirled around. "*Javla*

dum!" she muttered to all her sensational-looking Swedish friends and they all burst

out laughing as UG shuffled dejectedly past.

I was swimming in shame and embarrassment. I would never be as beautiful as

Elsa, or even Ingrid, her less pretty twin sister that sat next to her and bit the ends of

her wavy red hair. What was I *doing* here?

Finally, it occurred to me that I was thirsty and that a night of pretending to

smoke had made my mouthed parched. "Can someone pass the diluted orange juice?"

I asked to no one in particular.

Because it was a Reform camp and, therefore, lax in its adherence to Jewish

dietary laws[5], campers and counselors had the option of signing up for the kosher meal

plan. You had to fill out a form with your meal preferences every day like you were a

hospital patient and then hand it in to the camp cook, Johnny, an ex-Marine with a

scraggly mustache and a neck as thick as a cow's leg. He never left the kitchen except to

smoke a Marlboro Red. He'd chuck the empty packs in the dirt behind the kitchen. To

claim your kosher food you had to push your way through the dining hall, squeezing

past everybody else in line for bacon cheeseburgers and pepperoni pizza. You had to

ring a little bell and then Johnny would emerge from the back. He'd yank open a heavy

refrigerator door marked KOSHER, in bold red letters, and by the time you got your

Glatt[6] kosher turkey roll or whatever it was delivered in a truck each week from a

Hassidic butcher—the guys in the black hats with curly sideburns—in Crown Heights,

New York, you'd pretty much lost your appetite.

Great, call out the kosher kids, I kept thinking. *Hi, I keep kosher! No pig for me!*
No milk mixed with meat! It was more humiliating than being kosher in a room full of

Evangelical Christians. Nothing is more embarrassing than being more Jewish than all

the other Jews around you.

"You don't eat bacon?" somebody asked.

---

[5] Unlike other branches of Judaism where you have to follow God's word verbatim, the Reform movement doesn't stress total adherence to Jewish law, so there's a lot of leeway to eat whatever you want.

[6] If meat is Glatt kosher, the lungs of the dead animal are smooth, without any blemishes.

His name was Seth Cohen and he was sitting at the breakfast table across from Dev and next to me. Seth went to SUNY Binghamton. Seth was squat. Seth had pale skin and tufts of red hair on his shoulders that you could have gathered in twin ponytail holders. God knows why, but Seth wore tank tops. He was the exact carbon copy of Esau in the picture book Bible that I had as a kid. Seth had been going to Camp Kippewanscot since he was six and pretty much felt like he ran the place.

If summer camp was the Mafia, Seth was the capo, one rank below UG.

"Not usually," I answered. I didn't bother to explain the occasional Sunday night Chinese food outing.

"Ethical reasons?" he asked, narrowing his watery brown eyes. "Are you vegetarian?"

"No," I told him.

"Are you Orthodox?"

"If I were Orthodox," I said, "then why would I be at a Reform Jewish summer camp?"

"I have no idea. That's why I'm trying to get to the bottom of this."

"Bottom of what?" I asked. "I'm just Jewish. Plain Jewish. And I just don't eat bacon."

"Do you eat cheeseburgers?"

"Why does it matter?"

"Just curious. Do you eat cheeseburgers?"

"I've *eaten* a cheeseburger. With my friend Barrie. So she could piss off her parents who do keep kosher. Why don't you ask them—"

"So, you keep, like, partially kosher?"

"I'm just not eating the bacon, Seth. OK?"

"But why?" he asked. He leaned in closer, his breath a mix of American Spirits and Crest. "I don't get it."

This camp should have known better. They should have installed a salad bar with Tupperware containers of cubed ham on one side and brisket on the other with a mini mechitza[7] separating the two so that they never actually touched. And then Seth could have his nuked bacon and eggs and I could have my stale generic cereal and no one would bother me about any of it.

I wanted to call Barrie and scream at her until she punctured an eardrum. But she was in Thailand, sunning herself on a beach eating all the shellfish she could get her French-manicured hands on. I couldn't call anyone. I'd packed my cell phone charger and had forgotten in what bag, my cell phone was down to a single bar, and we were in the woods in the middle of Pennsylvania where there was no reception anyway. Until I could find my charger—rolled up in one of my fifty pairs of socks, because I don't follow packing lists—I was cut off from the outside world. My stomach tightened and I pushed my cereal to the side. I was never going to fit in.

"It's OK," said Dev. "I'm not into pig either."

---

[7] A partition that separates men and woman in the sanctuary of an Orthodox synagogue; in this case it would be more like a plastic divider, like in a refrigerator.

Something about Dev not eating pig made my heart beat fast. It wasn't just about pork. We were outcasts, he and I. Neither of us fit in. Mushy & Dev *versus* Camp. Mushky & Dev *versus* the World. I felt a trickle down my underpants. I clenched my knees together to hide my mounting excitement.

Dev folded his arms on top of the table. He stared down Seth, his hay-colored hair falling across one eye. "In fact," he declared, pointing at Seth's face. "I am a vegetarian. I never eat meat or shellfish. So when you think about it I keep more kosher than any of you." He turned to me. "Right, Sunshine?"

"Why do you keep calling me Sunshine?" I asked.

He did a quick look around the room. "Because you brighten up the place." He winked at me and did this clucking thing with his tongue that signaled that we were in this together. We were allies. He did not want to be here just as much as I didn't. His smile made everything safe. He reached across the table and tenderly stroked my hand.

And just like that, my fear of being stuck here all summer melted away like slices of Jarlsberg cheese on Glatt kosher hamburger patties bussed in from Boro Park, Brooklyn.

8:30 A.M. Clean-Up

"You look really, really, *really* cute," Dev said. "Really."

One more "really" and I might have died of embarrassment. I know people say that, but I literally felt a thump in my chest. We were standing on the sidelines of the soccer field, brandishing giant poster board signs above our heads. Mine read: GIRLS BUNK 1— KHATULIM. Dev's read: BOYS BUNK 10 —KELEVIM.

I was a cat. Dev was a dog.

Kippewanscot, in all of its infinite wisdom, had named the boys and girls units after the Hebrew words for domesticated animals.

We'd been baking in the hot sun for what seemed like hours as a steady stream of Greyhound buses rolled in with delivery shipments of campers from Monsey, Montclair, and Dix Hills. Dog and Fish and Bunny and Guinea Pig counselors all waited around, sweat dripping down our necks and onto our signs and onto our flip-flopped feet as it fast became clear that we would actually need to look after these kids. We would actually need to work. The shock was just beginning to sink in as I stared down at my t-shirt and drawstring sweat shorts.

"I don't look cute," I said to Dev. "I look like...*camp*."

The back of Dev's neck was glistening. His neck was thick, not as thick as Esau/Seth's trunk-like neck, but thick in an Irish-Catholic-South-Boston-Parochial-School-Football-Player-Matt-Damon-Mark-Wahlberg-kind of way.

"No," he said. "You look cute."

"No, I don't. I'm wearing my brother's shorts and a t-shirt from like three years ago." My eye caught a group of girls in petal pink Ralph Lauren tennis dresses. "I'm dressed worse than the campers."

"It's not how you're dressed," he corrected. "It's how you *look*."

"Well, I don't look cute."

He looked at me askance. "Are we arguing?" he asked.

Campers raced about the soccer field in a feverish pell-mell manner. None of them knew where they were supposed to go, despite the meticulous set-up of arrows and signs and camp staff flailing their arms and waving the campers toward their respective animals. Heads of brown and red and blonde whipped past like pool balls after a clean break.

Bored, Dev twisted his Claddaugh necklace around one of his fingers.

"How Irish are you?" I asked him, trying to change the subject away from how cute I was (n't).

"I'm not front County Cork if that's what you mean. I'm not Colin Farrell. I've never actually even *been* to Ireland. I've never been anywhere—"

"What about your family—aunts, uncles, grandparents or anything?"

He scratched his chin. Not a hair, just smooth skin. "My great-grandparents were born in Dublin. My mom was born in Woonsocket. You know, Rhode Island. Now she lives in Syracuse. Actually, a small town outside of Syracuse. Farm town about twenty miles north. Actually, it's not technically even a town—"

"So, you're not really Irish *Irish*—"

"*Mushky.*" Dev cut me off as a herd of campers charged toward us. He was definitely getting frustrated, which wasn't necessarily a bad thing. Guys kissed girls they were frustrated with all the time, especially girls they were frustrated with all the time. Perhaps I should frustrate him more. "I'm Irish," he said. "I'm Catholic. I was baptized. In a *church*. My mother prays to Jesus. Je.*Sus*. She doesn't know any Jews. The first Jews she ever met were the ones who go to my college. I know a lot of Jews, but my mother doesn't know any. I think she might actually hate Jews. She thinks Jews are going to hell because they don't believe in Jesus. I have not one single solitary Jewish relative. Not even close. Not even anybody that married someone Jewish. Not even anybody that has dated anyone Jewish. There are no Jews at all in my entire family. No Jews anywhere."

I liked that he kept saying *Jewish*. I wanted him to say it again.

On the field, campers whose parents had dumped them off at the Newark bus depot hours ago, halfway to their childless summer retreats on Montauk, had by now pretty much forgotten they had parents. It was a frenzied screech-jump-run-hug-twirl-around fest for the girls. The boys coolly waved to one another and immediately started up conversations about Rock Band and Wii.

The campers whose parents had driven them to camp moped around embarrassed, aimlessly pretending to be orphaned. Some of the younger ones clung slug-like to their parents, screaming and wailing like that scene in *Sophie's Choice* where Meryl Streep has to decide which of her children to sacrifice to the Nazis. I'd watched it with my parents. They were always making me watch movies about Nazis. Winter vacation last year they rented *Schindler's List, Europa Europa,* and *Au Revoir Les Enfants* all in the same weekend. Then they dragged me to see *The Reader.* And at the end of them all they'd yank me aside, look me deep in the eyes and say, "*See?* This is why it's so important that you marry someone Jewish." And I'd be like, "Why? Because Meryl Streep is a genius of an actress who won an Oscar for her strikingly convincing performance? Because Ralph Fiennes fell for Kate Winslet in old age make-up? Because they're all characters in movies and I'm living in real life and even if I did fall in love with someone that's not Jewish that doesn't mean I'm going to just stop being Jewish. Do you think you meet somebody who's not Jewish and suddenly...*poof!* Your Jewish self just vanishes into thin air and a non-Jewish alien descends down from outer space and inhabits your body like in a sci-fi movie?" And they'd usually shrug and ask where we should go to grab dinner.

We'd been standing on the soccer field for two straight hours. The sun beat down on my back. I pressed down on an area of leg and watched it blanch and then turn to pink. So far, I only had one camper. She was sitting cross-legged on the chalky foul line looking sullen and morose, her mouth pressed into a scowl. She refused to tell me her name.

Dev looked at me, and out of nowhere he asked, "Are you a...virgin?" He whispered the word like it was a venereal disease.

"That's a pretty rude question."

"I didn't mean to be rude—"

"No," I blurted, ashamed that he might think I were a virgin. "Of course *not*. What—why? Are you?"

"Mushky," he said. "I'm *twenty*."

Dev had two campers so far, two freckled brunette boys jaunting around in front of us, wrestling one another to the ground. Sullen Girl glared up at me, her amber eyes narrowing in glowering increments.

"Was it, you know, a positive experience?" he asked.

"That's not really any of your business."

"Really? I figured you were the type of person who didn't mind talking about stuff like that."

"What makes you think that?"

He shrugged. "I don't know," he said. "You just seem, I guess, honest."

"To people I *know*, yea. But we just met." But something about him made me want to tell him, made me want to tell him everything. I said nothing for a moment and then something inside me gave. "We met on one of those family tours to Israel." Of course, then I realized Dev had no idea what one of those family tours to Israel was.

"Israel," he repeated.

"Israel. You know, the country."

He rolled his eyes. "I know what Israel is, Mushky."

"Anyway, he was a famous child actor," I lied. "He'd had all these big roles on TV and in movies. It was mad, mad love. He wrote me letters all year and begged me to come visit him and I flew to California so I could see him."

Dev raised his brow, two bushy but very much separate bars of baby blonde. "You flew three thousand miles to get laid," he said.

"No," I corrected him. "I flew three thousand miles to lose my *virginity*."

Sullen Girl stared up at us. "So what was the guy's name?"

It would be the first in a long series of distractible summer camp romance moments. There would always be a camper in the way.

"What's *your* name?" I asked Sullen Girl. I'd already asked her six times.

"Why?" she asked.

"Because we're going to be living together for the next eight weeks."

"So?"

"So," Dev said, "it will make life a whole lot easier if we don't always have to refer to you as little shit—"

"So don't," she interrupted.

"Don't what?" asked Dev.

"Don't refer to me."

Dev and I looked at one another. I'd been a counselor for twenty-five minutes, and already I was a colossal failure.

"She'll find out anyway," he said. He grabbed the bunk list from my hand and wagged it back and forth in front of her. "Ashley, Ashland—"

"Whatever," Sullen Girl snarled, her gaze steadily fixed on a blade of grass that she was slowly and meticulously peeling apart. I wondered if she had mental problems. I did a quick flip through a stack of health forms UG had given us and found one girl in the unit with epilepsy, three with "asthma," and one with "ADHD," but nothing that

met Sullen Girl's sour disposition.

"I don't care if you don't like me," said Sullen Girl. "I don't even want to be

here. I wanted to go dig irrigation ditches with a radical leftist youth group in

Guatemala. But my parents got pissed off because I ran away from home this winter

and checked myself into a Comfort Inn for two days with their credit card. Camp is my

punishment."

Across the soccer field parents were frantically scampering around, folding

notes into envelopes marked with their child's name, enclosing lists longer and more

intricately detailed than the Swedish instruction manuals to IKEA toys. MANDY NEEDS

HER EPINEPHRINE SHOT. RUSSELL NEEDS HIS ASTHMA INHALER. HANNAH WETS HER BED. JOEY

HAS TWICE WEEKLY SKYPE SESSIONS WITH HIS PSYCHIATRIST. THIS IS NOT TO BE PUBLIC

KNOWLEDGE.

Eventually, parents and camper sorted themselves out. Parents fell to one side

of the field and headed toward their cars. Campers fell to the other side where they

made their way toward us. It was the parting of the Camp Kippewanscot Red Sea,

campers and counselors looking dumbfounded in that way people on a blind date do

after realizing they have to spend the next few hours trying to come up with things to

talk about. This blind date was going to be eight long weeks.

I fixed my eyes on Sullen Girl. She was fastidiously working on her second piece

of grass when Rochelle my co-counselor appeared.

Rochelle Rudnick wore platform sandals with DKNY jean shorts and 3-carat diamond studs in her ears and a tiny diamond tennis bracelet and a yellow gold nameplate necklace where the "R" was larger than the rest of the letters and encrusted with tiny pave diamonds. She was eighteen years old and from New Rochelle, New York, which she claimed was pure coincidence because she'd been born in Cherry Hill. She'd arrived late—something about traffic on the way back from the Hamptons where she'd been working on her pre-camp tan. Rochelle had gone to Kippewanscot as a kid, her aunt had gone, and her mom, so regardless of what she did, no matter if she skipped instructional swim or stayed out past curfew or lit fire to the sports equipment shack, she would never get in trouble. Her heels made clacking sounds against the basketball court as she made her introductory approach. She was a summer camp mafia wife in the flesh. I half expected an MTV reality show camera crew to be following her around.

"Hi," said Rochelle, extending her perfect, pink-manicured hand. "I'm Rochelle." She arched her back and shoved her training-bra A-cup boobs forward and angled her necklace towards the sun like it was a reflecting board. The idea of sharing a bunk with her for two months didn't exactly thrill me.

"Mushky," I said and shook her hand.

Rochelle liked it right away. "*So* cute," she said. "So good to meet you. What did I miss?"

"We're rounding up our campers," I told her. "This one refuses to tell me her name."

Rochelle peered down at Sullen Girl, arms akimbo, hands pressed against her slim hips. "What's your name?" she asked.

"Margot." Sullen Girl gave me the finger.

"I really need a bathroom," said Rochelle, fanning her pink baby doll t-shirt. It had a rhinestone-encrusted challah and the words CHALLAH BACK above it. "I'm totally shvitzing. I need a tank top. Has anyone seen my trunks? I sent two via UPS a few days ago."

Dev rolled his eyes. Rochelle glared at him. "What's your name?"

"Devin," he said. "McGillicudy."

"Cool." She was totally unimpressed, but polite about it. Dev was neither Jewish nor obviously in medical school, so she had no reason to socialize with him. "You smoke?" Dev and I shook our heads. "OK, then." She drew a pack of Menthols from her back pocket and smacked it against the side of her spray-tanned upper thigh. "I need a cig' fix. See you guys at the bunk."

Rochelle waved goodbye. Sullen Girl followed. As Rochelle clomped away across the basketball court I was sort of amazed that a 105-pound girl with a concave chest and legs the width of a ski pole could make a clacking sound as loud as the President's security detail. Rochelle's sandals were so thunderously loud I hadn't even noticed that ten campers had manifested on the soccer field in front of me, expectation flickering in their eyes.

It was hard to distinguish one from the other. French braids ran into pigtails ran into ponytails ran into powder blue and hot pink eye shadow smudged across each girl's lids.

There was only one that stood out. She was five feet tall and had way bigger boobs than I did and a faint butterscotch blonde mustache (All summer long, she'd secretly pluck it while the other girls were sleeping). She wasn't quite fat but definitely not un-fat. She wore a fitted orange t-shirt that said BOCA RATON. Her mother, standing beside her, bore a large net sack filled with pink grapefruits. They were a walking mockery of the sunshine state, a human postcard on a rotating rack at Publix.

"They're for the bunk," she said, handing the grapefruits to her daughter. It was hard to keep my eyes off her iridescent coral pink lipstick. Her white Capri pants hugged her rounded hips, and her sandals were metallic gold with a large fake pearl on each buckle. Her boobs were as big as the grapefruits. "Fresh from Florida. Picked from our yard."

Dev bit his lip to keep from laughing.

The mother yanked me aside. "Ruth might get her period," she warned me in a raspy nicotine-seasoned whisper. She pointed to Ruth, standing sadly while holding the bag of grapefruits. "We packed her with a box of maxi-pads just in case."

She kissed her daughter. "Have a great summer," she said, waving as she waggled off on her high-heeled sandals, her hips sashaying from side to side.

Ruth peered up at me with glossy eyes and a wary grin. The other campers were huddling around me, tugging on my shorts like kittens scratching at a mother cat.

56

Dev's campers, dirt smeared across their cheeks and t-shirts, punched him for attention.

I looked at Dev. "What am I supposed do with them?" I asked.

"I have no idea," he shrugged. "I was just thinking the same exact thing."

Uncle Stan rolled across the soccer field on his golf cart waving like he was riding a float in the Macy's Thanksgiving Day Parade and shouting directions through a bullhorn. I deciphered the phrases, "upper camp," "lower camp," "right," and "across the lake," but I was unable to string them together in any logical sequence. Luckily, my campers knew the routine, pulling me by my shorts.

Dev's campers yanked him in the opposite direction. "Hey," he called out to me as the gap between us grew wider and wider. "I was just sort of wondering—what kind of guys do you usually go for? I mean, do they have to be Jewish?"

Dev had blonde, blonde hair, wore a Claddaugh around his neck, had pale blue eyes and wore a muscle tee with a picture of a mustang on it. I wanted him, just as he was. But of course I couldn't tell him that.

My response echoed across the soccer field: "Yes. Jewish guys. Nerdy, hot Jewish guys who wear glasses, have mounds of unruly chest hair and dress in Oxford shirts from J.Crew."

9:00 A.M. First Period

Dev showed up the following night to the camp-wide welcome dance wearing

a button-down shirt, horn-rimmed glasses and a beat-up ZBT fraternity baseball hat

squished atop his head.

"Where did you get that?" I asked, squinting at the hat.

"The shirt?" he said, tugging at the collar. "I had this."

"Not the shirt."

"Oh, the glasses? I usually wear contacts—"

"The hat," I said, squinting at the Z, B and T. "Where did you get the *hat*?"

ZBT—Zeta Beta Tau— was a national Jewish fraternity popular with popular

Jewish guys popular with popular girls in Jewish sororities. At Harvard and Tufts

where Barrie would sometimes drag me on weekends to roam the bookstores and the

campus Au Bon Pain, scouting for prospective boyfriends to prepare for what she

coined, "our future M.R.S. degrees," the ZBT guys showed premature signs of male

pattern baldness and drove pastel blue Mercedes with vanity plates that said MYBENZ

and FLUBYU. They all wore New Balance sneakers and pastel button-downs and spent

Christmas vacation at their grandparents' condominiums in Sunny Isles, Florida.

"The hat is mine," said Dev.

"You mean a friend gave it to you."

"No," he said. "It's mine."

"Come on," I said. "You're lying. You borrowed the hat to go to camp to get Jewish chicks to sleep with you."

"I need a hat to get Jewish chicks to *sleep* with me?" Dev scrunched up his nose, which was large and aquiline and, come to think of it, did look a little Jewish. If John F. Kennedy had an affair with Dustin Hoffman, that would be Dev's nose.

"Wait—" I cocked my head to the side and pursed my lips in thought. A lot of guys I meet have a hard time believing that even though I skipped a grade and got a perfect score on my PSATs, I'm actually pretty dense. "You're *in* ZBT? Really? But you're not—" My eyes immediately went to the area below his belt.

"First non-Jewish President ever." He brushed a stray piece of grey lint from his shirt collar. It fluttered in the air and landed on my metallic blue Havaianas flip-flop (metallic blue was hot that summer). Dev picked it off my foot, his finger skimming my toes. He blew the lint into the air.

"You're President of ZBT?" I asked. "Honestly? For real?"

"I thought you were a genius and they let you skip ahead in school?"

"I'm not a genius," I said. "I'm just a really good test taker. If you were a multiple-choice question I'd probably get you right."

"You think too much," Dev said. He cast me a sidelong glance with his bright, lapis lazuli eyes, the kind of blue that gets bluer and bluer the longer you stare at them. The blue in Dev's eyes was endless, as bottomless as the unplumbed depths of the ocean. Right now, I felt like I was drowning.

"It's strange," Dev said. "You seem pretty smart and yet it never occurred to you that I was just a guy who was in a fraternity who had the hat. It must be exhausting being you."

Suddenly, I thought about Lizzie Appelbaum. Lizzie was my old babysitter when I was a kid. She was always listening to awesome music, had hair she'd never cut that went down below her butt and never wore a pair of jeans that looked bad on her. Going into her senior year of high school, Lizzie's parents sent her to Israel to a yeshiva—it's a school where you study Torah and Talmud all day— in an effort to tear her asunder from her Rastafarian boyfriend who never used deodorant and played drums in a band. In Israel, they were hoping she'd meet a nice Jewish boy, but instead she fell in love with a Druze named Mohammad. They lived together in a tiny community north of Haifa and a few years later, they got married. The worst part about it was that the Rastafarian boyfriend landed a record contract with Warner Brothers and wound up converting to Judaism to marry a senior record executive. Lizzie's parents still haven't forgiven her.

"I'm not doing this to get back at them," Lizzie swore to me on a return trip to the States a few months after her wedding. "Mohammad simply *gets* me more than any other guy I've ever met."

"You get me," I said to Dev.

A DJ was spinning country western music. I assumed that because Dev was Irish and Catholic and from a small hick town that wasn't even really a town that he would try and get me to two-step around the rec hall and that would be the end of my short happy crush on him. But it was far, far worse.

"God," he said. "I hope they play some Kelly Clarkson."

"Kelly Clarkson," I repeated.

"Yea, Kelly Clarkson." He raised a light blond brow. "You don't like her? I've watched every single episode of *American Idol* since it premiered. Kelly Clarkson is a musical genius. She's this generation's Pat Benatar."

Thank God. He was gay! My romantic conundrum was solved.

"I'm not gay," he said.

"I never said—"

"No, seriously. I'm really not. I get that all the time."

"I believe you. It's just…isn't Pat Benatar this generation's Pat *Benatar*?"

"Really," he repeated. "I'm not gay. I'm like the least gay person you'll ever meet. I like Kelly Clarkson. And I'm man enough to admit it. And I think that if a person can't admire someone's musical ability just because she was on a reality show, well, then that's just shortsighted. "

I wasn't sure what to say. It was tragic, no matter how you spun it. I just prayed that he didn't like Justin Bieber. Or the Jonas Brothers.

"I like Kelly Clarkson, too," I said. "She's got an amazing voice, no doubt about it. It's really no big deal." But my heart sagged a bit and I stared down at the floor.

"What other kind of music do you like?" he asked.

There was way too much twang and way too many fiddles pumping through the loudspeakers, and way too many allusions to bars and beer bottles and pick-up trucks.

"Not country," I said.

I'm not sure why Jews don't like country music, but I think it might have something to do with us not owning guns or drinking Pabst. And I suppose it doesn't help that cowboys, as a collective ethnic group, have never been oppressed, not unless you count the backlash from the Marlboro Man cigarette smoking campaign. And you need pain in your collective historical experience for your music to have a groove.

Jews like Hip Hop. And Elvis. And Marvin Gaye. And Bruce Springsteen. And the Beatles. And if you're over sixty, Doo-Wopp. And if your parents haven't done a proper job of exposing you to all that stuff, then you like Rufus Wainwright and The Shins. Or you like Jeff Buckley and Elliot Smith and Nick Drake and a bunch of other suicidal dead people. And if you insist on liking music that kids your age are listening to, you dress up like a transvestite and play "Bad Romance" by Lady Gaga forty times on a loop. But no country, never country, not even if your iPod blew up and all of your downloaded songs were destroyed, never to be retrieved ever again. Not even if you were stuck in a Reform Jewish summer camp in the middle of central Pennsylvania where the only available music to listen to was country crap spun by DJ Blake, a British counselor who wanted so badly to be American he wore baseball caps backwards and walked around saying, "That's so awesome!" Americans might be stupid, but there is nothing more stupid than a foreigner trying to act American.

"I hate country, too," said Dev.

Four more of the sexiest words ever spoken by a Gentile.

DJ Blake cued a Carrie Underwood song and a group of red neck counselors from Texas began square dancing. A girl in a side ponytail donned a pair of denim Daisy Dukes and boots that can only be called shit kickers. A few of the Swedish counselors huddled around DJ Blake begging him to play European techno music.

"Do you want to dance?" Dev asked me.

"I don't know," I said. "I'm not really into Carrie Underwood. I mean, I appreciate her musically—"

"She's one of my favorite *American Idols*," he said. "She's not country, not really. She's really more pop cross-over." He sighed. This was going nowhere. "You want to get something to eat?"

I nodded enthusiastically. We navigated our way across the dance floor, bumping into campers that were twisting their angular bodies awkwardly to the beat. At the snack table, Dev poured two plastic cups of bright red beverage with fruit slices floating in it. He plunked ice cubes in each cup and handed me one. Then he dug his hand into an aluminum bowl filled with potato chips and dropped a few in my hand.

"So, are you still in love with him?" he asked, popping a chip into his mouth.

"Who?"

"The actor. The one in California. The one you flew cross-country to sleep with."

I could have lied again. There was a lot of potential that summer for pretending that I was a completely different person. I didn't know anybody, nobody knew me. I could have spent eight straight weeks being someone that I wasn't.

"No," I said. "I'm not in love with him."

"No?"

I hesitated a moment. "We never were," I confessed. "Losing my virginity was actually a pretty miserable experience."

"How so?"

"There was a Feist song playing. And he sent me home in a taxi—"

"God," he said screwing up his face. "That is bad."

"I know," I said. "It made me feel like a hooker or something—"

"Not that," said Dev shaking his head. "The music. Feist. She sucks."

"She doesn't completely suck. But that's not really the point—"

"She *sucks*. She's probably the least talented singer out there."

"Now you're scaring me," I said. I crunched a chip hard. "Next thing you're going to tell me is that you've got a poster of Taylor Swift above your bed."

"Above my desk," he said. My heart sank Titanic-like to the bottom of the pop music ocean. "Her music really speaks to me."

"What does it say?"

"*Everything.*"

I felt like I was going to vomit. "I don't feel so well," I said, fanning my loose-fitting blouse. It was turquoise and didn't really go with my flip-flops but I didn't care.

64

I dressed for comfort, not for Dev. I didn't want to be one of those eight-year-olds on the dance floor that was already matching her socks to her underpants. "It's really hot in here."

I took my punch and sped off, finagling my way through dancing campers. Dev followed. "What's wrong?" he asked.

I stopped short on the dance floor. A group of gyrating girls dressed in fluorescent leggings nearly stampeded me to the ground. "Taylor Swift?" I said, my stare hard and cold.

"So we have different tastes in music," he shrugged. "So what? It's just music."

I furrowed my dark brown brow. "Just *music*?"

Dev smiled, his chipped tooth peaking out beneath his plump upper lip. "You're funny," he laughed. "You get so wound up over the smallest things."

"Music isn't *small.*"

"Look," he said, resting his hand upon my shoulder, its soft warmth little consolation for the fact that I was growing ever more certain that aside of the eyes, the hair and the smile, there was little—maybe nothing—that could sustain my nascent affection for him. A guy can't be hot if he's got lousy taste in music. He just can't. I don't care who he is. "We can talk about other things," he brightly suggested.

"Like what?" I asked.

"I don't know." The right side of his mouth pulled up into a sharp curve. "*Sex?*"

You can tell a guy likes you if he keeps bringing up sex. This was well-known fact and didn't make me a genius. But standing there I somehow feel privy to information about boys that I hadn't quite understood before. I was determined to show Dev that I got what he was doing, I got his little game, and if he wanted me to play along, then he was going to have to try harder.

"Ok," I said. "So talk."

"Me?"

"If you want to talk about sex then talk about sex."

He pulled me by my arm across the dance floor to a semi-circle of chairs. We sat down. "Ok, well—" He paused. "I can tell you this. The first time is never good."

"No," I agreed.

"I mean, I was with Sinead for seven years and the entire first *year* we had sex it was downright awful. We didn't know what we were doing."

"Sinead?"

"I mean, we were thirteen and consumed with Catholic guilt and thought we were going to hell—"

"Like Sinead O'Connor?"

"Sinead Sullivan. We met in parochial school when we were ten."

"You lost your virginity when you were thirteen?"

"She's married to a dentist now." He guffawed a little. "Jewish guy."

"That figures," I said.

"She's very happy," Dev said a bit sadly. "But, see, it never would have worked with us. She dated that guy for a month before they got engaged. That shit doesn't happen when you're fifteen, sixteen."

"Not unless you're Romeo and Juliet. Doesn't Taylor Swift sing a song about them?" (Frightened that I knew this.)

"'Love Story.' Best. Song. *Ever.*" I swallowed hard. "Anyway," he went on, "I think it's actually better *not* to be in love with the person you lose your virginity to, because the chances of you ending up with that person are pretty slim."

"But isn't that kind of pessimistic?"

"No," he said. "It's optimistic. Why would you want to find your one true love before you've gone off and lived life a little bit? You're first time with famous actor guy, you said it was bad—"

I nodded. "Pretty bad. I mean, even aside of the Feist thing."

"Well, that's good. You've gotten the bad first time out of the way. So the next time can only be amazing." Something across the room caught his eye. "Wait here," he said. He popped up, headed toward DJ Blake and left me solo in my chair. And that's when Brian Bluestein came over.

"Hi," he said, extending his large, bony hand. "I'm Brian Bluestein." His skin was thin, stretched hard across his knuckles, and for a moment that's all I could focus on. He sat down in the empty chair beside me.

"I'm Mushky," I said to be polite.

"I'm Brian," he said again. "I go to Harvard."

"I go to high school."

"That's cool. You thinking about college applications yet? It can be so confusing. All those essays they want you to write. I applied to like fifteen schools before deciding I wanted to go to Harvard. If you need any advice or help or have any

questions—"

"Yea. Maybe. I was thinking about Yale."

"Yale's great. I got in there, too. But I got more money from Harvard."

"Wow. That's really impressive."

He chuckled. He was twenty-one years old and had a face that shaped like a

triangle. He wore oversized glasses and had a twitch in his left eye. He had ample black

hair on the back of his neck and arms, but was balding up top. He had really straight

teeth and his lips were as thin as a pencil tip. He was wearing a t-shirt that said I DIG

ISRAEL. In short, he was a Jewish mother's dreamboat. Somewhere up in heaven, my

Russian Jewish great-grandmother was grinning. *Choose him! Choose him!*

"I'm head of culture," he said. "My elective."

"Yea?" I asked. "Like Jewish culture?"

"Apparently," he began, "it's one of the least popular electives at camp. Last

year there were only three campers enrolled all summer, and only because their first,

second and third choices were all taken. The only elective less popular is Israeli dance.

Last summer it only had two campers. The Israeli dance instructor cried."

"That sucks." I said. "What do you teach exactly?"

He smiled at me. Perhaps I was the only person at camp so far who took an

interest. "I haven't really figured it out yet," he admitted, staring down at his bright

white sneakers (They'd stay clean all summer because he never did any sports). "I'm

majoring in civil engineering with a minor in Near Eastern Studies, so maybe…." He paused, scratched his forehead. "I just got back from an archeological dig in the Negev Desert—I could show them pictures, I guess. And I speak four languages. You want to know what they are?"

"Sure." I did, actually.

"English, obviously. French, Hebrew and Arabic."

"That's pretty cool. My Hebrew is not so great."

"I could help you," he said. "I'm actually publishing portions of my senior thesis in *Harper's*. I wrote parts of it in Hebrew. And I've got this really cool position worked out for winter break this year interning at the Israeli Consulate—"

And that's when Dev came back. And my Russian Jewish great-grandmother's smile imploded into a tight frown. *Stay away! Stay away!*

"Hi," he said, peering downward at Brian.

"This is Brian," I said. "This is Dev."

Brian and Dev shook hands. From across the room, Dev motioned to DJ Blake. A few seconds later, he stopped playing country and cued a Britney Spears song. This wasn't going well at all.

"Now do you want to dance?" Dev asked me. His golden hair looked feathery under the moody blue lights of the rec hall, his eyes as translucent as a fresh mountain stream. *No!* Shouted my Russian Jewish great-grandmother. *No! No! No!*

"Yes," I told him, and as he took my hand and led me to the dance floor I swear I could feel the weight of Brian Bluestein's heart sagging on the chair behind me.

Dev's touch sent a tingle down my neck. The tingle inched down my chest and deep into my cleavage where it burrowed for the entirety of Britney's three-minute-eleven-second bad boy anthem "Toxic." Everyone was fast dancing around us, but Dev insisted we link body parts. He placed his hands on my zaftig (Yiddish for chubby) Russian-Jewish ass (my ancestors needed it for padding during the long, cold Muscovite winters), molding my denim-covered flesh in the palms of his sturdy, Irish workman's hands (My own stereotyping at work; I assumed he could fix cars). My body curved toward him as though pushed by a current of wind. I felt shy and embarrassed and weird, but also good, grown up, like a college girl. It was as if that dance when I was twelve and mistaken for a hot boy that looked like a Jonas Brother never even happened.

I refused to look Dev in the face. I'd danced with a few boys, but not like this. I'd done it with stiff, outstretched arms, feet squared, legs slightly apart as though aiming for a spot on the ground to pee. I'd bounced furiously around a dance floor with Ben Katz on the disco boat cruise around the Sea of Galilee where they played "Barbie Girl" by Danish pop-rock group Aqua, but our dance was clumsy, impersonal, indifferent. We pretty much avoided one another. This kind of closeness, with hands on my ass, was all new to me.

I fixed my gaze on a group of girl campers across the room. They were my campers and they scared me to death. Ruth was standing beside Ashley (I think that was her name) who stood beside another Ashley, or maybe it was Erika. I-think-her-name-is-Ashley wore a *Twilight* t-shirt that said EDWARD and with a picture of a translucent-skinned Robert Pattinson. Another Ashley/Erika wore a similar shirt except hers said I LIVE FOR JACOB and a picture of the swarthy actor who plays the werewolf. Whatever their names, they were collapsing in laughter as they watched me dance with a boy.

Mushky's got a boyfriend! Mushky's got a boyfriend!

"Do you know all your campers names?" I asked Dev.

"God, no," he said. "I tell them apart by their bedspreads."

Knit one, pearl two, Mushky and Dev, woo-hoo!
Knit two, pearl one, Mushky and Dev had some fun!

"Mine are Margot. And Ruth. And Mandy. Samantha. Ashley, Erika, *another* Ashley—"

Maybe her name wasn't Ashley. Maybe it was Ash*land*. There were so many new trendy names that summer – there were four Madisons in the same bunk – it was hard to keep track. Long gone were Sarah, Rebecca and Rachel. Jewish girls' names had gotten so gentrified. She wasn't in my bunk but there was actually a girl at camp that summer named Sun Moon Rain Rosenfeld, which I thought was trying way too hard.

Mushky's got a boyfriend! Mushky's got a boyfriend!

I saw my Russian-Jewish great-grandmother's face and my head started to spin.

"I feel sick," I told Dev and I darted off the dance floor and out the rec hall.

Dev gave chase, following me outside to a bench where we sat beneath a sickly-looking tree with grooves in its trunk and half its leaves missing. The tree looked sad, displaced, like it was stuck in the wrong season. Planted at camp like me when it should have been in a forest somewhere.

"I'm not supposed to be here," I said, dropping my chin into the palms of my hands. I watched a mosquito nose-dive into a citronella candle.

"With me?" asked Dev.

"At *camp*."

"Where are you supposed to be?"

I thought of Berkowitz. We'd made plans to spend a week at his cousin's beachfront house in Malibu. We were going to hang with a few of his friends from high school. He was probably there right now, sand caked on his back, hair salty wet, splashing around in the same yellow-and-blue swim trunks he'd worn the day we snapped photos of one another floating in the Dead Sea raising newspapers above our heads. I could be with him right now. But instead, I was with a guy with hair as fair as Goldilocks and a Claddaugh necklace around his neck and a ZBT baseball that confused everything.

"Why are you *really* here?" I glared at Dev, growing bolder by the second. "How could a guy in college not have anything better to do than go to summer camp?"

"You overestimate college."

"There were no other jobs?"

He looked at me, his eyes softening. "Truth?" he said. "I really needed to get away from my family."

"What's wrong with them?"

"My mother's great. My dad—" Dev fidgeted a little. "He bailed when I was three. My mother sort of never—well, I'm all she has. I love my mom. She's the greatest woman in the world, even if she thinks Jews are going to hell. I don't know what I would do without my mom. But, you know," he sighed, "it can get pretty fucking exhausting taking care of her."

It was pretty sweet and pretty disarming. I'd heard about Jewish boys being secretly in love with their mothers, but I had no idea that this phenomenon extended into the Irish Catholic community as well. "That must be very difficult," I told him.

"It's my life," he shrugged. "What about yours?"

"My family?" I thought about my mom running out for dishtowels at Marshall's and my dad tucking into a plate of vegetable fried rice at Yang Chow. "I don't know," I said. "They're...normal, I guess."

"That's OK." He said it sort of conciliatory. Maybe I was wrong, but I sensed he was disappointed. "There is one thing," I said. And it just came out. "My cousin is dying."

Shelli, my twenty-three year-old Israeli cousin, was really sick with lung cancer. I'd only met her six or seven times but we'd grown up writing letters to one another. She was skinny and had a shock of red hair and wore stacks of silver and gold bangles on her long bony arms. She smoked cigarettes in front of her parents like it was no big deal. She came to visit us one winter during her break from the Israeli army and took me shopping at a thrift store in Cambridge to buy spangled skirts and ballet slipper flats. The last time I'd seen her was during the summer trip with Berkowitz. She snuck us into a Tel Aviv nightclub where she got drunk and told us that she was maybe going to die.

"I'm sorry," Dev said. "Are you close?"

It was weird knowing somebody around your same age that was going to be dead soon. It made me feel guilty about worrying about stuff like what was going to happen to me when I got older. Or whether or not Dev was ever going to kiss me.

"Kind of," I said. "We email a lot and mail packages and stuff to one another. She's only twenty-three. Six years older than I am." I examined the lines on Dev's hands, tiny rivulets forming an "M" shape on the fleshy part of his palm. "Three years older than you."

Dev reached out to touch my tangle of long, brown curls. He brushed a flyaway strand from my face. I hardly ever shampoo my hair because there's rarely any point. No matter how much conditioner I slather onto my head, hard, lumpy knots form at the base of my skull, and when it rains the curls break out in runaway frizz. I'm seriously surprised a bird has never tried to lay an egg in my hair. No boy—no person, not even me—has ever, *ever* been able to successfully run his hands through my hair. Not even when it's wet.

"You've got great hair," said Dev. "It's amazing. I want to live in that hair. I want to smell it. I want to hold it against me as I sleep."

"You sound ridiculous," I said. "Stop it. You sound like a bad song."

"You've got great lips." He traced them with his forefinger. I flicked it away.

"What are you doing?" I asked.

"Nothing," he said. "You're beautiful."

Two of the sexiest words ever spoken by a Gentile. Three if you count the contraction.

"Dev," I said. "Don't kiss me."

"Why?" he asked.

"And stop touching my hair. And my lips."

"But why?"

"Because..." *Because you're not Jewish. Because I'll disappoint my parents. Because my Russian-Jewish great-grandmother's hardened expression is looming large in front of me calling out, "I survived decades of religious oppression and violent attacks of anti-Semitism so you could run off with a goy?"*

"Because there's someone else," I told him.

Dev wrinkled his nose, as though the idea of it was just preposterous. *"Who?"*

"He's a good friend. His name is Berkowitz. We met on that family vacation to Israel I was telling you about. He's one of my best friends and when we both get older and we're ready to get married—"

"Married?"

"When we're ready and mature enough to settle down—"

"Hold on a sec," said Dev. "Where is this Berkowitz guy now?"

I scanned the area around us. There was grass and rocks and trees and a vast expanse of inky darkness through which mosquitoes dipped and darted. No Berkowitz anywhere.

"In California," I replied, staring glumly at the nighttime sky.

"Look," Dev said, "I get it. I was sort-of-kind-of dating this one girl for a few months before summer—"

"What was her name?"

"It doesn't matter. Jennifer."

"That's not a very original name."

"She wasn't a very original girl. I mean, she was OK. She was smart and funny and even kind of beautiful. But it doesn't matter. Because I broke it off."

"Why?"

"Because I wasn't quite sure about her. And I was coming to camp. And I didn't want to be tied down to someone in case…"

"In case what?"

Dev looked into my eyes. "In case I met somebody that I *was* sure of." He grasped a fist of my hair and gently massaged it back and forth between his palms. I was going to make him stop but then something miraculous happened. Dev did the impossible.

He finger-combed my hair without his fingers getting snagged in the knots.

10:00 A.M. Second Period

Rochelle decorated the wall above her bed with magazine clippings of the

world's top supermodels, an idolatrous collage of supermodel icons with body parts

marked like a "before" shot on *Dr. 90210*. With disconcerting precision, she took a

black permanent marker and circled on each model's body the parts that she most

coveted. Gisele Bündchen: boobs, shoulders, tumbling waves of honey-colored hair

(Tom Brady standing off to the side in a "Startracks" snapshot from *People*). Natalia

Vodianova: eyes, legs, nose. Kate Moss: a faux fur coat with ballet flats and Top Shop

shorts from a paparazzo photo in *Us Weekly* magazine. And because she's Israeli and

blonde (living proof that Jewish girls can look like Gentiles without having to get one

of those Japanese straight perms), Bar Refeali (She circled her entire body).

I was convinced that Rochelle's dad must be a plastic surgeon. Either that or

Rochelle —"Ro' the Ho'" was her nickname in junior high— was a deranged psycho-

killer plotting a mass murder of the modeling industry.

Turns out, Ro' just liked models. And her dad was one of Rockland County's

most sought-after OBGYN/fertility specialists. Per Ro', J.Lo had booked a visit

following a miscarriage at seven weeks and Julia Roberts had popped in for an

appointment when she was pregnant with the twins and experienced a first trimester

spotting scare while on location for a film. Rochelle knew which celebrity had fertility treatments and who had conceived naturally. And none of them had conceived naturally.

"Infertility is the new bulimia," she informed me on our first night as co-counselors. "And pregnancy is the new black."

I assumed she meant black as in the color as in the Little Black Dress as in pregnancy is on trend. But she actually meant black as in people, as in, "Angelina made adopting black babies very popular, but now getting knocked up through in vitro is the new adopting black babies."

She also tried to convince me that smoking while pregnant wasn't as bad as they say, one of the many questionable obstetrical facts she'd dictate throughout that summer. "It can contribute to low birth weight," she pointed out, "but given our country's huge obesity problem, don't we *want* our babies to be skinny?"

I kept thinking, If Barrie were here, she and Ro' would become best friends that hated one another and talked about one another behind one another's backs.

As for my own bunk bed, I hadn't committed to as fantastical a decorating job. I'd packed a stack of books (most of which were on the required reading list for senior year Advanced Placement English); a Moleskine journal and a new package of pens; a picture of me and my parents and Bucky snapped at his bar mitzvah party with the four of us on the floor doing the bicycle-pedal move with our legs in the air as the band played "Shout" from *Animal House*; and a shoebox filled with letters from Berkowitz. I'd taped the picture on the wall, placed the books and writing materials inside a cardboard Target three-drawer dresser, and slid the box of letters under my bed. I propped my iPod with its playlist of old 70's and 80's songs up on a shelf. My forest green flannel bed spread from R.E.I. looked institutional against Ro's striped satin sheets from Bloomingdale's.

Peering around at my campers' bunk bed areas, I thought I'd for sure disappointed them all. There were *High School Musical* posters and framed glossies of Zac Efron and Vanessa Hudgens above each girl's bed. Ruth pushed a quilted padlocked case filled with maxipads and tampons underneath her bed. Erika—and if you called her Erica she'd get really mad at you because there was a huge difference and she could tell—had a plucked sample of Lindsay Lohan's pubic hair that she swore her lawyer father had procured through a colleague who had represented the drug-addled starlet during one of her D.U.I disasters. And they all had these purple and pink furry journals with felt monkeys and sparkle peace signs and the words CAMP COOL, LOVE BFF, SLEEPOVERS and SHARE A SMILE from the chain store Justice.

The only one that didn't have a fuzzy diary was Margot who, for whatever reason, still insisted on giving me the silent treatment. Above her bed of black flannel sheets she tacked a poster of a white skull and bones. Beneath her bed stood a stiff pair of black, knee-high combat boots, even though it was June and we were in the middle of a heat wave in central Pennsylvania.

And then there was Mandy from Minnesota. Mandy and her second cousin Samantha lived in St. Louis Park, an upper middle-class suburb outside Minneapolis (they filmed bits of *Juno* there, she proudly told us). Their parents split a lake house time-share in the Poconos, which is how they wound up at a camp in Pennsylvania.

Mandy was petite and pretty, but Samantha scared me a little. She had budding B-cups (her boobs weren't disconcerting D's like Ruth's, but Ruth was shaped like a pear) and long legs and long, wavy whiplash hair. She sat on her bed and folded a tiny red string bikini then gingerly placed it in her top dresser drawer. I'd only brought monochromatic one-pieces in blue and grey and black. Marveling at the itty-bitty bathing suit, I placed my hands on my zaftig ass, imagining it getting larger by the minute. I padded around from bed to bed, trying to act all enthusiastic and muster up as much current pop cultural knowledge as I could, but my campers were not easily taken. My parents' one grave mistake in raising me is having not pushed me more to like things that other kids my age liked.

"Do you like Ashley Tisdale?" asked Ashley (from Westport). Not to be confused with Ashland (from King of Prussia. I'd finally learned the difference between the two; King of Prussia had a mall).

"Sure," I said.

But when Ashley unrolled two different posters, with two vaguely familiar blond actresses that looked strikingly similar but with two different noses, I uttered my first in what would be a string of unforgivable pop cultural mistakes: "Who are they?"

Ashley recoiled. "They?"

"They're movie stars, right? I think in that Disney—"

"Um, *High School Musical*?"

"Right."

"Um, are you joking?"

I shook my head. "What do you mean?"

Ashley and Ashland clutched their stomachs and chortled. They huffed and tossed back their matching manes of pony-brown hair. "You are so stupid!" They shout out with such sinister pleasure I felt near certain they'd have their parents ring UG and demand me banished to a YMCA day camp with communal showers somewhere in inland New Hampshire.

"It's the same actress," snapped Ashley, her fiery eyes darting back and forth. "One of the posters is before she got a nose job!"

"That's right!" I exclaimed, pretending to have known all along. But on the inside I was sobbing. I would be skinned alive this summer if I didn't quickly pad my deficient résumé with more tween reference points.

"How many times have you seen HSM?"

I did the quick acronymic math in my head. High. School. Musical. "Twice," I said. "No, three times."

"We've seen it, like, ten times," said Ashland. "And the second and third ones like…" She counted on her fingers that were painted with cherry red nail polish. "Like twelve!"

I didn't want to lie to them. I wanted to tell them the truth, that not only had I never seen HSM One, Two or Three, but that I was heading into my own senior year of high school and, while I didn't know much about the HSM trilogy aside of Ashley Tisdale's nose job, most of my classmates at school were depressed, confused, or on heavy medication for something. Nobody sang or danced in the hallways. The movie they all loved was a lie.

But I knew if I told them that they'd hate me forever. I was going to have to work harder for my campers' affection than I'd worked for anything ever—grades, national merit scholar awards, writing competitions. I had to convince them that I was cool.

So I meekly asked, "Do any of you read books?"

Ashley and Ashland cocked their heads in unison. "Duh!" scoffed Ashland. "Of course we read!" She charged over to her bed, grabbed a stack of soft cover books with glittery purple covers and shoved them at me. Each one had a bold block-letter title: BOYFRIENDS, GIRLFRIENDS, and EXES. "I've read every book in the series," Ashland proudly announced.

I suddenly got sad and depressed about the copy of *Middlemarch* that I was supposed to read for my AP English class. I would never admit it aloud, but EXES looked a lot more interesting.

"George Eliot is cool," I said to them, trying desperately to hold my own. "She was a woman who pretended to be a guy so she could write really boring thick books about 19th century England."

Ashley's and Ashland's eyes turned scarily blank like they had absolutely no idea what I was talking about. I'd bought a *People* magazine at the airport with Ashlee Simpson and her new boyfriend on the cover and, thinking fast, handed it off to

Ashley. "I read *People*," I offered meekly. "Look, your name. You know, except with an
–ee."

"Cool," said Ashley/Ashland (by now it was obvious they were a pair and would
never be further apart than the size-2 waistlines of their matching terry cloth miniskirts). "Who do you have hanging above your bed at home?" They asked, all fluttering
eyelashes and flushed pink cheeks.

I desperately tried to think of someone age appropriate. But the truth was that
the only guy that I had hanging above my bed was Bruce Springsteen, a guy in his 60's.
A guy my parents' listened to. A guy whose concert my parents, with feathered hair
and sleeveless t-shirts, attended in 1984 (they showed me photos). I'd been into Bruce
since I was seven, when my second cousin Michelle came over for New Year's Eve and
while our parents partied upstairs, we locked ourselves in my bedroom and sat cross-
legged on the floor and memorized the liner notes to "Darkness on the Edge of Town"
(we'd swiped the CD from my parents' car) which we thought made us the two most
awesome people ever since everyone else at school was into music sung by kids who
didn't have any pubic hair. We were retro which made us cool.

"Who?" asked Erika, whom I had an urge to call Erica and piss her off but, for
obvious reasons, couldn't. She squinted at me hard.

"Springsteen," I repeated. "He's a singer. Your parents probably listen to him—
or your grandparents. He wrote a bunch of post-September 11th songs that aren't half
as good as his early stuff but still lyrically promising in their own right."

Malina Saval

"We were only three when September 11th happened," Ruth cruelly reminded me.

Only Margot knew what I was talking about. "He's old," she said sharply. "He's on the cover of *Rolling Stone* every time there's a political election. He wears a jean jacket and has facial scruff and an earring. You've probably heard your grandparents sing that 'Born to Run' song when they get stoned and think you're sleeping."

There was a faint flicker of recognition, a few nods here and there. But mostly, they all thought that I was a freak.

"Celebrity crushes work on an exponential curve," I tried to explain. "You're eleven, so you like guys that are seventeen. When you're twelve you'll like guys that are twenty. When you're my age, you'll like guys that are—"

"Dead," said Margot.

The others screwed up their faces, distraught by the whole idea.

"I still don't get it," said Mandy. She cocked her head to the side and looked at me askance. "Are you sure you're...*normal*?"

I wasn't. And then the girls started to sing. And I sort of knew the words from Camp Ruach, and I tried to sing along, but the tune was different and I had a bad feeling that I looked a lot like Dev when he attempted to mouth the blessing before the meal:

> *We're from Khatulim*
> *And no one can be prouder*
> *And if you can't hear us*
> *We'll yell a little louder!*

Luckily, just then, Ro' sprung from her bed: "Let's play some icebreakers!"

We sat down in a circle on the bunk floor and linked hands. "OK," said Ro'. "We're going to play the Tell-Me-A-Secret-That-Begins-With-The-First-Letter-Of-Your-Name game." She folded her hands in her lap. "I'll go first. My name is Ro' and I like to run—see, that's an 'R'— around my house naked."

Samantha went next. "My name is Samantha and my...*sister* Roxanna doesn't know that I found her pack of birth control pills in the top drawer of her dresser."

And so on.

"Next game," said Ro'. "We're going to each try and guess what color underwear the girl next to us is wearing. Someone guess me."

"Red—"

"Blue—"

"White—"

"Yellow—"

"Purple—"

"Wrong!" exclaimed Ro'. "I'm not *wearing* any underwear!"

After Taps that night, Ro' sneaked out to smoke cigarettes. She wound her way carefully through the trees to a secret shrub-covered spot down by the lake and leaned against a rock while flicking her ashes into the marshy shallows. I watched her through the tiny slat in the bunk above my bed.

Ro' puffed and flicked her way through the first few nights of camp, tossing her head back to blow rings of smoke into the muggy, mosquito-infested air like a bad B-list actress in an Italian foreign film. From the start it was clear that Ro' was going to be the counselor that did no work, but that all the girls loved. They would pen long missives home begging their parents for a babysitter just like Ro', someone to teach them how to French kiss a pillow and dress like a hooker for evening activity. And I was going to be the one with boy briefs (grey) and a stack of boring Victorian era novels and a crush on a rock legend in his 60's. I'd bust my big fat zaftig Jewish ass to pull off this job.

And fail miserably.

If camp was the mafia I was nothing but a low-ranking thug. I could be killed at any moment.

—

Dev was sitting on the grassy knoll by the volleyball courts. He was wearing Adidas sneakers and a classy green t-shirt that said IRISH YOGA with cartoon figures sprawled supine on a bar floor surrounded by empty beer bottles. I'd seen that exact same shirt in the window of the Right Aid outside Fenway Park on a display rack next to the Styrofoam ice coolers and plastic beach chairs.

"Hey, Sunshine," Dev said, without looking to see if it was me. His back was arched toward the sky like a model in a suntan lotion print-ad.

It was the first week of camp and our bunks were paired up for daily activities. Specialty electives (such as Radio, which I was still head of despite the fact that I had no idea what I was supposed to teach) had yet to start, so the idea was to give each camper a 15-minute taste of such titillating, mind-blowing activities as Israeli Dance (The counselor teaching it was Hadar, an Israeli girl with hair under her armpits who wore Grecian sandals and long, gossamer skirts through which you could see her g-strings and pubic hair—everyone called her "Hairdar"); Newcomb (I was sure the sport was the stuff of urban camp legend but apparently it existed); arts and crafts, sailing, ceramics, field hockey, softball, tennis, rock climbing, canoeing, catamaran, windsurfing, horseback riding (My fear of heights kept me sidelined but Dev showed off his cantering skills on a stallion); soccer, singing, gymnastics, drama and touch football (We touched!).

But we still hadn't kissed.

Things didn't get truly uncomfortable until fourth period swim on day three.

"You look beautiful," said Dev as I passed by in my belted black tank.

I was standing on the dock with a towel wrapped around my waist and my bare feet in a puddle of lake water. I liked the thinning effect of the suit's spaghetti straps on my arms and the way the twisted bandeau top squished my boobs together for extra cleavage. But as Samantha shimmied by in her tiny red bikini and took a jumping leap into the lake, I was certain that Dev was mocking me.

"I knew you'd look *good*, " he began, "but you seriously look…"

"I do not," I said.

Dev was too cool for a swimsuit. He wore jeans and a tank top. Kind of like the burnouts in gym class who wore jeans and t-shirts during the required one-mile run when everybody else was in shorts. His Claddaugh charm sparkled in the sun.

"No, really," he said. "You look...." He eyed me up and down, squinting as if to zoom in on specific body parts. "*Amazing.*"

I clamped my towel even tighter. "Stop it," I told him.

"I mean it," he said. "If you don't mind me saying so, your breasts are..."

My face turned the color of an extremely not kosher Alaskan crab. "Dev—"

"The most amazing breasts that I have ever seen in my whole entire life."

My breasts were not as terrific as Ruth's and we both knew it. I yanked my towel up to my neck and glanced over at Ro'. She was on the far end of the dock, sunning herself in her rhinestone-studded hot pink bikini. Everything about Ro' was rhinestoned. Even her pedicure had tiny fake stones on her big toe. She'd forged a note on her father's medical office stationery that said she had "acute *mittleshmerz,*" painful ovulation that lasted up to two weeks at a stretch and required her to sit out swim. I told her this was dumb and pointless since ovulation only lasted about 24 hours so there was no way anybody with ovaries and an I.Q. above fifty was going to believe her.

"Lake water is bad for my skin," she insisted. "I don't want some camper drowning and anyone expecting me to dive in and save the kid. Anyway, nobody at camp will even know what *Mittleschmerz* is. They'll know it's a German word and that it sounds like something truly awful as all German words do. They might even think it has something to do with Nazis." She'd sit out swim all summer.

"Our first counselor's night is tonight," Dev said to me.

"Yay." I pretend pom-pom-ed the air.

"You're not itching to get out of this dump?" he asked. "I figured you'd be dying for a clean getaway."

"I am," I said. "I'm just not that excited to throw down dollar beers while listening to LeAnn Rimes on the radio at the local watering hole."

I pointed in the direction of the long dirt road that lead out of camp. It was three-quarters of a mile, and partially paved, but something about the way it started out wide and then gradually narrowed until it emptied out into the grassy camp parking lot left me feeling claustrophobic. In Hebrew school when Barrie and I studied the story of Passover, we learned that the Hebrew word for Egypt, *Mitzrayim*, meant "narrow." Pharoah, the ruler of Egypt, was narrow-minded. Enslaving the Israelites was narrow-minded. So far, this camp felt like Egypt to me.

"What's wrong with LeAnn Rimes?" asked Dev.

"I have nothing against her personally," I told him. "I kind of like that song about her not knowing how she's going to live without him. I don't even mind all that much the twang in her voice. I just have this aversion to singers with capital letters in the middle of their first names."

Dev nodded. "That's interesting," he said. "Uptight and ridiculous, but interesting. I could play you some of her new songs. They're not getting much radio play but I think the b-sides are more listenable. She's really hit her stride I think since divorcing that back-up dancer."

"Look," I sighed. "I'm just getting used to the whole Kelly Clarkson thing. Can we talk about something else?" I thought about the Bruce and the Bob Dylan on my iPod. Jewish or not Jewish, this was never going to work out.

"Have you even listened to Kelly's last album?" Dev asked. "Because it's really— "

"OK," I said. "Fine. I'll go to the stupid bar and learn how to square dance with all the Texan counselors."

"Relax, Sunshine." He tugged playfully on my towel. "We don't have to go to a bar."

"Well, where else am I going to walk?"

"You don't have to walk," he said, his azure eyes twinkling in the sunlight. "Because I've got a *car*."

The four sexiest words ever spoken by a Gentile at a Reform Jewish summer camp in the middle of godforsaken nowhere.

—

Dev's Camaro convertible was shiny and black and had a bra stretched across the front hood that was even bigger than Ruth's Wacoal double-Ds. I was happy that I'd worn jeans. Barrie had told me this one horror story about a girl who'd gotten into a guy's vinyl-upholstered convertible during a summer heat wave. Her sweaty thighs got stuck to the seat and patches of fake leather got stuck to her skin and they had to be scraped off surgically at Mass General.

90

"You look adorable," Dev said. He was wearing khaki shorts and his ZBT baseball hat smashed down on his head, his buttery locks curling up around the rim.

"Look," I said, digging the heel of my grey Converse sneaker into the grassy parking lot (I'd purposely worn shoes difficult to slip off). "This isn't a date."

Dev shrugged. "OK."

"Seriously. Not. A. Date."

"I said OK." Dev smiled. "You really look pretty."

"I'm in jeans," I pointed out, as if he hadn't noticed.

"So?"

"So I made no effort not to dress up. Because it's not a date."

"Mushky," he said. "We're at camp. I wasn't expecting a cocktail dress."

"Because it's not a date."

"Not a date."

"We have nothing in common except the same-age campers and first period volleyball."

"Third period—"

"Not a *date*."

"Got it."

He got in the car and turned the key to the ignition. I flung open the door to the passenger side and propped myself down on its sticky vinyl seat. I yanked down on the seat belt and tugged it firmly across my chest. I clicked the seatbelt in its buckle like I was strapping on a machine gun.

"This can not go *anywhere*," I told him.

And we didn't. We drove in circles for an hour trying to hunt down an eating establishment that didn't have the words MOOSE or BEAVER in its name. There was road kill on every restaurant sign from Mount Pocono to Mountainhome. On enormous, multi-colored murals, caricature-like cartoon animal eyes stared out from bloody, larger-than-life sized burgers and steaks, as if the food were having a laugh at the expense of the poor dead animals. Earlier, Ro' had informed me that anytime she went out with a boy she always ordered the side salad with lo-cal dressing ("You can't *ever* let a boy know you eat."). I was starting to see her point. But I was also getting hungry and Dev didn't know where the hell he was going. One thing about me is that I've never trusted anybody's ability to get me anywhere. As we passed a ramshackle take-out joint named ANTLER ANNEX for the second time in twenty minutes, my heart slumped. I suddenly wanted to be back at camp.

Dev had Kelly Clarkson's "Since You've Been Gone" — or at least I think that's what it was called since she kept screaming it over and over and over again—blasting on the car stereo. We drove around so long that I found myself tapping my foot to the beat. My stomach was rumbling. I'd picked on bland camp food for days but now I missed it.

"I'm starving," I said, but Dev didn't respond, his eyes peeled on the road. I looked at my watch. "We've got to be back for curfew in two hours."

"Take it easy," he said, taking a random turn-off. "Can't you just enjoy the ride?"

"Enjoy riding around in circles listening to angry break-up music?"

"Is this a break-up song?" Dev asked, raising a butterscotch brow in a way that suggested he was dead serious. "I always considered it Kelly's way of telling a boy that since he's been gone she actually really, really, really misses him."

"No" I said, shaking my head. "I am not going to sit here analyzing Kelly Clarkson lyrics like she's John Lennon. I mean, she's good, OK? I admit that she's got some serious pipes but—"

Dev rolled his eyes. "Maybe you should be a little more open-minded—" He stopped mid-sentence. "Look!"

Seventy-two minutes in the car and there we were, parked in front of a rainbow of electric blue, hot pink and lime green neon signs, the light from them reflected in puddles of dirty hose water on the cement below. A calliope sounded steaming whistling notes against the cacophonous backdrop of amusement park rides. Overhead, a rollercoaster cranked its way up, down and around rickety wooden curves.

"Cool," said Dev, "a carnival."

Growing up, my parents never once took us to a carnival. I'm not sure what it was, but there was something about semi-permanent exhibitions and collapsible fried dough stands that they averted at all cost. We went to Disneyworld, once, in fourth grade when I was nine. My father bought a three-day pass. We spent Day One at EPCOT because my father thought the World Pavilion with all its faux international flavor was more intellectually stimulating than "It's a Small World" and souvenir snapshots with Mickey. On Day Two we stood in line for three hours for Space

Mountain and then Bucky threw a fit and we never wound up going on it. On Day

Three we piled into our Chevy Malibu rental and my father drove clear across state to

Clearwater Beach where we sat on terry cloth towels that we bought at Eckerd and ate

tuna fish sandwiches wrapped in cellophane. We never made it back to the Magic

Kingdom. Our Disneyworld Grand Passport stated in tiny fine print that entrance was

good for a lifetime, but that was the last time my dad took us on a family trip anywhere

that required standing in line for more than five minutes.

Then in sixth grade, our local USY chapter organized a field trip to an

amusement park in Rhode Island. On the flume ride, as we flew down the big finale

hill, I smashed my chin on the front part of the log. My two bottom teeth cut right

through my upper lip and blood gushed everywhere. The chaperone on our trip was

too dumb to realize that I needed actual medical attention so she sent me alone to the

First Aid stand behind the haunted house ride where some gangly kid with a buzz cut

and a bored look on his face handed me a Bandaid. That was the last time I went to an

amusement park.

"I want everything," Dev said. "I could eat the Ferris Wheel."

We skipped in the direction of a little white stand with a sign that said

HOMEMADE CANDY APPLES. We ordered four slices of pizza, a large side of fries, two

super-sized Cokes and a giant basket of onion rings. For dessert we got fried dough

and a half-dozen chocolate chip cookies. We ate it all sitting on a bench in front of the

Scrambler, where "You Never Met a Motherf**cker Quite Like Me " by Kid Rock

wailed as ride-goers were jerked around in jewel-colored carts.

Dev watched me eat. He had this way of running his hand hard through his hair the way some people smile when they're feeling confident. "I like that you're not afraid to eat in front of me," he said, peeling off a string of melted cheese from my lip.

"Please stop looking at me," I told him.

We took a spin on the Ferris wheel. The ride was packed and we were squished beside a fat woman with circles of underarm sweat on her baggy floral top.

"This is pretty romantic," Dev said.

"Oh, dear," said the fat woman, pressing her palm against her fleshy pink cheek.

We were dangling from the apex of the Ferris wheel, our cart swaying back and forth as ride-goers boarded down below when Dev's iPhone rang. The first few notes of the *American Idol* theme music blared from his cell. He looked at the CALLER ID and let it ring until it stopped.

"It's my mother," Dev said. "She likes to call on Sunday."

"Oh," I said. "That's sweet."

"You know, when she gets back from church."

"Oh. That's sweet."

"She likes to repeat the priest's sermon and make me feel guilty because I'm not at church."

"So how come you didn't pick up?"

"I will when we get off the ride," he said. "She's really into Jesus."

"You told me."

"She's got this Jesus figurine on the wall above her bed."

"You mean a crucifix?" I asked.

"Not a crucifix," he said. "It's not of Jesus dying. It's just of Jesus."

"Cool," I said. "That's really…spiritual." As we rotated our way back down to the ground, I visualized Dev and I having sex in a bed, a giant Jesus figurine hovering overhead. And then the ghost of my dead Russian-Jewish great-grandmother would descend upon us and hurl a bowl of ice-cold Borscht at Jesus.

The fat woman beamed, clasping her hands together, bursting with excitement:. "I go to church every Sunday!" she squealed.

Back on land, Dev's iPhone rang again. This time, he answered.

"I'll be right back," he told me, cupping the iPhone in his hand. As he stepped away and crouched beside a ride with the word SIZZLER and killer pythons painted on its side, a curious thought spun through my head: Gentile boys don't call their mothers—*do* they?

As Dev spoke in whispery tones, his iPhone pressed against his velvety blonde sideburn, I made a list in my head of all the pros and cons of letting Dev kiss me:

Pro: He's hot. Con: He went to parochial school. Pro: He's smart. Con: My parents would disown me. Pro: He's got his own car. Con: It's a Camaro.

Dev hung up. "My mom is all alone," he sighed. "It's hard for her, you know? She's got nobody. Sometimes I feel so bad about leaving her. Turns out, she needs major knee surgery. And she doesn't have health insurance."

He took my hand, our sweat commingling in the viscous Pennsylvania humidity.

"You wanted to know why I'm working this stupid camp job?" he said. "It's because I *need* to. The job market sucks out there. I couldn't find anything else. And I need to make some money this summer. I need this job so I help my mother pay for her surgery."

Pro.

11:00 A.M. Third Period

It rained for three days straight—luscious summery rain, dewy and warm, pelting rhythmically against the bunk's slanted roof. Swimming, waterskiing and windsurfing were all cancelled (Ro' was thrilled; her *mittelschmerz* excuse was wearing thin). Canoeing and sailing were both relocated to the lifeguard shack where campers sat around on lifejackets studying Red Cross safety manuals and scrubbing oars with surf wax. All other outdoor activities were held indoors, which meant that sports electives became screenings of PG-rated movies and the arts and crafts shack was open all morning for macramé, bead-making, decoupage and other aesthetic diversions normally reserved for elderly white women living in upstate Vermont.

For days campers slugged through the muddy grass in colored jellies and knee-high rubber boots toting around lopsided ceramic pinch pots and coffee mugs that would likely be relegated to their parents' basements in marked cardboard boxes. I made myself one, "MUSHKY" pressed in fingerprinted lettering on the bottom of the mug and the date right next to it, as if someday that moment might become important. I didn't tell anybody, but I sort of liked in-door activities. I was getting paid crap, but I was sitting in an arts and crafts shack making a pinch pot. Which was way more fun than a real job.

For three days rest period was extended by 30 minutes to compensate for the camp's lack of creative rainy day programming. For each of those days, Ro' sat on her bed painting her toenails sparkly pink while flipping through the latest issues of *Elle*,

Lucky and *Vogue*. Erika, Ashley/Ashland and Ruth were all gathered goggle-eyed on

the edge of Ro's bed, listening with rapt attention as she imparted her expansive

knowledge of Brazilian models' first and last names, astrological signs, bra sizes, and

their birthplace down to the tiny Amazonian village hospital. She could even tell you

what sport they were playing or what mall they were skipping school to hang out at

when they got discovered. She ran down the list of model stats like they were Geometry

test flashcards:

"Fernanda Motta…Birthplace, Campos dos Goytacazes, Rio de Janeiro,

Brazil…Birthday, January 1, 1981…Height, 5'10"…Chest, 34 inches…Waist, 26

inches…Hips, 25 inches…"

And then every once in a while my campers would get bored of Ro' and break

out into a round of song:

> *I'm so tired*
> *Don't know what to do*
> *Somebody told me*
> *You were tired, too*
> *So, maybe, we can have a lazy day—*
> *Please!*

I tried to focus on *Middlemarch* but spent most of free period staring out the

window screen where glimmering raindrops collected like miniature crystal balls,

wondering what Dev was doing over in Boys camp.

And then every once in a while my campers would get bored of Ro' again and

break out into a different song:

The Lord said to Noah:
There's gonna be a floody, floody
The Lord said to Noah:
There's gonna be a floody, floody
Get those children out of the muddy, muddy
Children of the Lord

Can I be honest? The songs weren't half bad. I would have taken one of those

over a Taylor Swift tune any day.

Electives began. Each afternoon, for fifth and sixth period, as rained thumped

down on camp, I was holed up in the radio shack with no idea what I was supposed to

teach and an old shortwave radio that could supposedly contact Russia but that neither

I nor any of my campers could figure out how to work. So we listened to my iPod

("Radio" was clearly an antiquated elective that no one had bothered to update in the

summer camp catalogue) that I hooked up to two small speakers that I managed to

borrow from Margot.

"If you break them I'll string your bra up on the flagpole," she warned me with

a murderous look in her eye. She'd finally begun communicating with me with

incendiary fighting words and not just dirty sidelong sneers. I was breaking through.

My camper was threatening to string my undergarments up a flagpole. She was paying

attention to me. This could only be a good thing. I wasn't a total failure after all..

"I won't break them," I told her.

"I'll cut off your hair while you're sleeping with the pair of scissors I stole from

the art shed."

"I won't break them."

"I'll sprinkle itching powder all over your bed and rub poison oak all over your pillow."

"I won't break them," I repeated for the third time. "But if you do any of those things to me—if you do *any* of those things to me—I'll spread a vicious rumor around camp that you attended a Miley Cyrus concert in a full-on Hannah Montana costume."

I got the speakers. In the radio shed I played set lists with songs by Bruce Springsteen, Marvin Gaye, and John Lennon. No Kelly Clarkson. No Carrie Underwood. No musical artist that had ever won a recording contract on a TV show. I gave them a real musical education in 60's, 70's and 80's rock and old school R&B that my parents, despite their myriad other pop cultural flaws, had done with me. I got them singing "Born to Run" by the end of day one. My first true camp counselor victory.

That same day at that same time, Dev was in the computer shack directly across from radio. Every few minutes, he'd poke his head out the window, mouth "Hello," and smooth his bangs that fell in buttery diagonal wisps across his forehead.

At dinner that night one of Dev's campers raced breathlessly to my table and pushed a folded note into my hand. "It's from *Dev*," he droned boyishly.

It was a M*A*S*H note. Dev and I lived in a house, in Brazil, we had seven kids and we drove an Aston Martin ("without a bra"). The arrangement held a lot of appeal. We could live in a beach house in Rio de Janeiro, I could wear a g-string (because once you hit the sand at the Copacabana you grew long, whiplash hair and a perfect heart-shaped ass) and we'd hang out with Gisele when she was in town with Tom Brady and the kids. Maybe Ro' could swing by for a stay and open up a Brazilian jean bar.

The rain grew more aggressive. And so did Dev. He sent boy messengers cross-camp delivering missives, poems, and a card he made in arts and crafts with glued-on foam paper hearts and the words BE MINE in pink and red sparkles.

Then he turned up at optional Saturday morning Shabbat services.

"What are you *doing* here?" I asked.

There were five of us on the screened-in deck where boys camp head counselor Darren bunked for the summer. The rain had washed out the camp-wide apache relay race, the all-camp outdoor ice-cream mixer and the season's first inter-camp tennis tournament between Camp Kippewanscot and Camp Tel Noar. Upper Camp—campers fourteen and up—was in the rec hall watching *Zombieland*. Lower Camp—kids seven to age thirteen—was watching *Toy story 3*. But I was feeling a strange twinge of homesickness. I missed my bed, I missed TV, I even missed Barrie. Maybe getting into God would help, and if not, there were the rumored herring slices on waxy plastic plates they supposedly served for Kiddush.

But I wasn't exactly expecting Dev to be standing there in his ZBT baseball hat, hunched over a bent-open prayer book, poring over an English transliteration of the Sh'ma[8]. Dev took off his ZBT hat and there it was—a yarmulke. A black, papery one gathered in a pointy triangle atop his mop of soft blonde hair, lopsided and ill fitting,

---

[8] The cornerstone prayer of the Jewish peeps, affirming our belief in one God. Typically not recited by blonde Irish Catholic boys in Claddaugh necklaces.

but a yarmulke all the same, the same kind of yarmulke President Bill Clinton wore at

Yitzhak Rabin's funeral (My mother was fond of showing me the *Jerusalem Post*

newspaper photos: "Such a *good* friend to the Jews," she cooed).

"Shalom," said Dev.

"Is this a joke?" I asked.

"You don't like my yarmulke?"

"It belongs to the camp."

"It's communal."

"Dev," I said. "Your name is Dev. *McGillicudy.*"

"And?"

"And you're at an optional Shabbat service. Key word—*optional.*"

"Look around," he said. He scanned the small deck where three others sat

around on fold-out chairs spearing herring slices with toothpicks and sipping

lukewarm Manischewitz. One of them was Russell Simchovitz, the gaunt, red-headed

summer camp rabbi who was pursuing his rabbinical degree at Hebrew Union College

in Cincinnati. "Aside of me—and we know *I'm* not Jewish—only four Jewish campers

and staff are here," Dev pointed out. "Not a very impressive showing for the

community if you ask me."

He was right.

"So what—you're going to convert?"

He shrugged. "I don't—"

"Because that's pretty presumptuous. One lousy service at a Reform Jewish summer camp does not a Jew make."

"Dude, can you relax—"

"Like suddenly you can identify with me on that level?"

"I never said—"

"So what are you doing?" I asked. "Because you're starting to act a little crazy."

"I'm not doing anything," said Dev, "And you're the one acting crazy. And if I were you, I'd be happy, or maybe even excited, that someone not of faith took an interest in my particular religion."

"Why would that excite me?"

"Because," he said, holding his prayer book in the air, his piercing pools of sky-blue peering intensely into my dark brown eyes, "You like me. I can tell, even if you won't admit it. And I even kind of get your whole little thing about you being Jewish and me being Catholic and that Berkowitz guy, or whatever his name is. But you know what? None of it matters. Or it shouldn't matter. Because I'm starting to really, *really* like you. And isn't that what matters the most?"

—

That night after Taps, half the counselors stayed in the bunks and the other half went out to a local bar called Buckeye (It was all decided by unit). I didn't have a fake I.D. (Barrie had promised to arrange for one before dumping me for Thailand) but there was no way I was going to go with the other underage counselors bowling.

There were only six of us counting Ro', and she warned me that if I went bowling and my campers found out that it was because I hadn't gotten into the bar, they would think that I was the biggest loser on the entire planet and make my summer a living hell (as if so far they had made things easy). So I took my chances at Buckeye.

Over the bar's entrance was a flickering red sign missing its "u" and its "B" was cracked in half, rain swatting it as if a tinkering reminder to get it fixed. Ro' pulled me by the arm past the bouncer, a burly, bear-like figure with a shaved head and a full growth of beard, a bunch of tats on his arm—guns, a dragon, the American Flag—and a t-shirt that read I SUPPORT THE TROOPS. He could have lifted us up one-handed and tossed us across the parking lot. But instead he let us in.

"It's my red Bobby Brown lipstick," declared Ro', loudly smacking her lips. "Works *every* time I need to sneak into a bar."

The floor was flaked in sawdust and the pool table's top was all torn up, dusty cue sticks blunt from decades of heavy camp counselor use. Music played—a thumping bass— but you could barely make out the lyrics above the clatter of the crowd. A waitress curled around tables carrying a tray of frosty Heineken bottles, and I overheard snippets of a conversation between two regulars debating what bar served the best malt scotch and something about bait tackle shops.

Ro' made a beeline for a group of toe-headed townies that was gathered around the jukebox knocking back shots, and left me standing alone. Dev was at the bar, so I sat down next to him. He was nursing a beer as pale as his hair out of a tall, cylindrical glass. I was never a big drinker (which is why I never really saw the point of getting a fake I.D), but tonight I wanted to be culturally supportive.

"I'll have a Guinness," I told the bartender.

Dev smiled, his teeth (except for the chipped one) perfect Chiclets of pearly white. The bartender slapped my drink down and I took a foamy, icy cold sip.

"I was just thinking," Dev announced, tilting back his glass, "about how much your people and my people have in common."

"What do you mean?"

"Jews. The Irish. We've both been oppressed. Take the potato famine of the late 1800's, for example."

"The potato famine and potato latkes are *not* the same thing," I told him.

Dev shook his head. "Where is your sense of humor?" he asked.

I stared into my drink, a cloud of foam floating atop amber liquid. "What about Jennifer?" I asked.

"What about her?"

"Was she upset when you dumped her?"

He wrinkled his forehead. "I wouldn't say I…*dumped* her. I just ended it."

"What's the difference?"

He thought about it for a moment. "I wasn't mean about it. I just told her I wasn't able to commit."

"But now you want to date me. Even though you can't commit."

"It's different."

"Why?"

"Because I didn't really feel that thing with her."

"What thing?"

"You know. That…*thing.*"

I wasn't sure why I was giving him such a hard time. I liked him. I liked him a lot. I liked the way his lips looked, all wet from his beer. I liked that he liked me. I liked wondering what his chest looked like underneath his t-shirt.

"Wait," he said. "Watch this." He pulled his iPhone from his pocket and began thumbing past pictures. He stopped at one and showed it to me. "This is my mother," he said. She was short, blonde-grey, and had blue eyes like Dev. She was wearing a cross around her neck and a purple housecoat and it looked like there was a barbecue in the background. "Memorial Day," he said. He thumbed past a few other photos until he got to one of a brunette girl in a miniskirt and tank top. "That's Jennifer," he said. Her hair was straight and she was skinny and had pretty small boobs. Not original at all.

"I'm deleting her," he said.

"Why?"

"Because I don't want her. I want you."

He clicked the DELETE button. And like that Jennifer evaporated into iPhone ex-girlfriend heaven.

"How do I know you don't have other photos of her?" I asked.

"Mushky," Dev sighed. "Why are you trying so hard to fight this?"

"Two reasons." I held up my index and middle fingers. "Mushky. McGillicudy."

"So you'll keep your own name."

"It's not the name," I said. "It's because—" I trailed off. What was it because of—my parents? Guilt? Embarrassment? Fear? I couldn't think of anything. I wanted him to kiss me so badly that my mouth started to ache.

"Forget it," I said. I drew a long sip and then slammed my beer down on the bar top. "You don't understand. And it's too difficult to explain without sounding like a bigot. That's why it's best to avoid dating non-Jews in the first place. To avoid these types of discussions."

"Don't yell at me," he said. "You're the one who wants to talk."

"What's that supposed to mean?"

"I didn't sit down next to you," he said, standing up from his bar stool and heading in the opposite direction. "You sat down next to *me*."

—

I couldn't deal with the bus ride back to camp. My stomach was twisted up in a sailor's knot and I was in no mood to be surrounded by a bunch of inebriated counselors in their 20's singing drunken rounds of elementary school bus driver songs. So I left the bar and followed the long dirt road back to camp, alone, in the rain, trying hard not to think about things. I looked at my watch. It was 11:35 PM. In twenty-five minutes I was expected back at my bunk, tucked in between my extra-long sheets on which Margot had likely smeared poison oak.

Suddenly, I was stopped in my tracks by a blinding flash of light. "Mushky," said a husky, female voice in the dark, her flashlight blinding my view of her.

"It's Janice," said the voice, now angling her flashlight at my feet. Janice was head counselor of girls camp. Her job was essentially to sleep in her own bunk, never attend any electives, and mosey around camp with a flashlight. Technically, her position put her in charge of overseeing all special activities, field trips and socials, but I never once saw her doing any of those things. When she wasn't holding a flashlight, she was holding a clipboard, the summer camp equivalent of General Petraeus. She was forty-two-years-old and had been going to Camp Kippewanscot since she was a kid. She was obviously avoiding the real world. She was at that stage in the mafia universe where you move into a nursing home in Florida and play shuffleboard and bingo, except she refused to go. She wore the same iron-pressed shorts and beige Birkenstock sandals every day, and t-shirts with liberal political slogans from various presidential eras. Tonight she wore a faded red one with the words THE ONLY BUSH I TRUST IS MY OWN embossed across the front. She had tight, wiry hair. She wasn't out of the closet, but everyone knew that she was a lesbian. I had an urge to run fast in the opposite direction.

"Mushky—" she faltered. She was wearing a yellow rain slicker over her t-shirt and her Birkenstocks were caked in mud. "We got a call from your parents earlier this evening." She spoke evenly, as though she'd been practicing. "I tried to get in touch with you, but you were already at the bar."

My heart started to twitch. "Is everything OK?" I asked.

"It's your cousin," Janice whispered.

"My cousin—Shelli?"

Janice gulped hard. "She died early this morning."

She extended her hand and placed it upon my shoulder. I wanted to hit her. I hated when people that I didn't know touched me. There she was, standing there in her dorky hippie sandals and ugly yellow raincoat and angry political t-shirt and touching me because my cousin that she didn't know had died. I hated her.

"Are you OK?" asked Janice, bracing her clipboard flat against her chest. The rain trickled down upon its faux-wood finish, making a loud clacking sound.

My body turned ice cold. It's a myth that when someone you love dies you burst into tears. I didn't feel like crying. The only thing I felt like doing was punching Janice in the face.

"Your parents boarded a plane tonight to Israel," she said. "They'll be arriving in the morning. You can call them then. They left their number."

"They didn't want me to go with them?" We'd talked about it, here and there, but we all sort of avoided the topic. Now, a jolt of prickly anger coursed through me. I was stuck at camp in the middle of nowhere. And my parents were on a plane to a country halfway around the world. I knew my parents, and they were practical people. They'd help bury my cousin and then head to a Tel Aviv beach snack bar for a falafel.

"They had to rush, the funeral is tomorrow," said Janice.

"I know that it's tomorrow," I snapped. "Jews bury the dead the next day. Well, unless someone needs to *fly* somewhere—"

"They didn't think there was any way you'd make it." She tried to assuage me but it did no good. "By the time we got you on a bus to New York and then a flight out of Kennedy. I'm so sorry, Mushky."

I hated Janice. If my parents had wanted me to come they would have found a way. But they didn't, because even though I was seventeen, they still had this ridiculous idea that death was something that I was too young to deal with. I'd stay at my camp, my brother would stay at his nerdy gifted and talented summer science program at Johns Hopkins and we'd forget my young, beautiful dead cousin Shelli come morning flag-raising. "They're *kids*," I could hear them say, flicking their wrists. "Why put them through all this?" As if not going made it all better.

Janice finally withdrew her hand. "If you need some time," she said in a drawn-out, unctuous voice, "I can take over your electives for the next couple of days."

I wanted to scream at her to leave me the fuck alone. I wanted this camp to disappear. I wanted to dissolve into tiny molecules and be sucked up by the sky so that I wouldn't have to spend one more second in this horrible, boring-as-all-hell-camp-in-the-woods-in-central-fucking-Pennsylvania.

"Fine," I said to Janice. "Whatever."

I turned and ran. I ran past the staff lounge. I ran past the rec hall. I ran past the nurse's clinic, the little white cabin stocked with Cepacol and cold remedies prescribed for every possible malady. I raced past the archery range, the cold rain slapping my soaked hair against my face. I ran past the soccer field and the arts and crafts shack. I ran past the tennis courts and the basketball court and burst breathlessly into boys camp. I stopped at the bunk with the brass number seven and a picture of a dog on its door and fell to my hands and knees.

"Dev!" I cried out.

For a moment he didn't come. I felt my heart stiffen, like someone was clamping it with a wrench. I picked up a stone and chucked it against the bunk. Then another. And another. I flung my body onto the ground. "*Dev!*" I called again.

He appeared outside in the t-shirt from the bar and boxer shorts. "Jesus," he whispered. "You're going to wake up all of boys camp."

I ran to him. Acid-hot tears mixed with rain burned my cheeks. I threw my arms around him, pressing my head against his soft, broad middle.

"What's wrong?" he asked, holding me tight against him, smoothing down my hair. "What is it, Sunshine?"

"Shelli…my cousin…she died," I whimpered.

"Oh, Mushky."

I loved it when he said my name.

I peeled myself away from him, staring at the spot where I'd left a wet dent in his t-shirt, my hair mashed up against my sweaty forehead. I looked at him, knowing that this was the moment that was going to change everything. He looked at me, like he knew it, too. And then I said it, clumsily, through sonic hot tears, almost choking on the words: "Life's too short to wait around for a Jewish guy."

You haven't been kissed until you've been kissed in the rain, at midnight, at summer camp, by the Irish Catholic Head of Computers.

12:00 P.M. Lunch

And like that, the rain cleared.

The days following were sunny, bright, barefoot weather. During rest hour,

campers scampered through the hot, scorched-grass soccer field in bathing suits and

cutoffs, pummeling one another with water balloons and squirting spray bottles at one

another's flushed naked faces to keep cool during the rising afternoon heat. They sang

and sang and sang, excited as ever about the sun like it was the first time they'd ever

seen it.

> The sun came out and dried up the landy landy
> The sun came out and dried up the landy landy
> Everything was fine and dandy, dandy
> Children of the Lord

It was the first week of July. We'd been at camp almost two whole weeks and

my campers had made fast friends with their fellow bunkmates. My heart softened a

bit and I was getting to like them. I actually got a kick out of studying them and all of

their quirky, funny tween ways. Cousins Mandy and Samantha mixed and matched

their bikinis. Samantha paired the top from her cherry-red one with boy shorts she'd

borrowed from Ruth; Mandy wore the cherry-red bottoms with one of Erika's designer

t-shirts. Even Margot got in the spirits of things, skipping her horse riding elective with

Ashley/Ashland and stealing a cigarette from Ro's pack of menthols that she kept

stashed in her underwear drawer.

Dev and I had been together four whole days, the summer camp equivalent of a silver wedding anniversary. Every morning at breakfast he'd sneak up behind me and trace his finger across the back of my neck. He'd whisper, "You look hot today," in my ear, even if I was in sweatpants and my hair was a tangled mess swept up in a rubber band.

Dev was there for me when I wanted to talk about Shelli. He read a draft of a sympathy card that I composed to her parents. He was there the night we were all sitting round the campfire and people started singing "I'm Yours" by Jason Mraz and my eyes started to water because that was Shelli's favorite song. He was there when I got sad and just wanted to sit there and not say anything. Religion never came up at all.

One afternoon, he sneaked up behind me and strung something around my neck. It was a copper necklace carved into the shape of a crescent moon. He'd painted it yellow, strung it on a leather cord and fastened it around my neck as I sat on the radio shack floor while my campers hijacked my iPod and forced me to listen to a brand new Demi Lovato song. It was the most amazing necklace that I had ever seen. It was so amazing I didn't even mind the song playing in the background or that Dev tapped his foot to the beat.

"This is a really great song," Dev said.

"Shouldn't you be teaching computers?" I asked him.

"Nah." He flicked his wrist and his downy blonde arm hairs tickled the back of my hand. "I taught my campers how to hack onto other people's Facebook profiles without having to add them as friends. They're obsessed."

"Is he your *boyfriend*?" asked Ruby. She was a plump 12 year-old from Bunny (*Shfana*) Unit who wore pigtails and Vans slip-ons with pink frogs on them and had multi-colored braces (Her dad was in Orthodontics). "Is he?" she repeated. "Is he your *boy*friend?"

It was annoying, but I'd have to get used to it. The word *boyfriend* at camp was forever italicized.

Dev looked at me, tilted his head and half-smiled. "Am I?" he asked. "Your *boyfriend*?"

I thought about it all that day.

And then again that night, after Taps, as Dev and I made out under the hot, bright lights of the basketball court.

And again the next morning in the dining hall as Dev pulled me gently toward him, buried his nose in my hair and put his hand in the back pocket of my shorts.

And again the next afternoon as Dev came up behind me during volleyball and whispered into my ear, "I bet you look beautiful *naked*."

Also in *italics*.

—

And then came Fourth of July.

Camp Kippewanscot put on its annual display of fireworks. A spectacular spray of colors exploded over the lake—red, blues, and whites erupting in a thunderous crescendo set to Gershwin music. Dev and I sat on the top row of the bleachers erected on the marshy bank, two dark silhouettes clinging to one another, making out, the moon's silvery reflection in the lake. We looked like a sappy commercial for the state of Pennsylvania Department of Tourism: *This summer you'll fall in love with Pennsylvania.* The campers weren't watching the fireworks—they were watching us. To our mutual embarrassment, the rousing round of applause at the end of "Rhapsody in Blue" on the camp-wide stereo speakers was not for the fireworks. They were for me and Dev.

The next morning, UG ushered us into his office. Dev and I stood next to one another, feet apart, heads slightly bowed, hands folded behind our backs, kind of like the way Brad and Angelina stood whenever they made a joint public appearance to promote *Mr. and Mrs. Smith* before announcing to the world they were together.

"We've fielded a hundred phone calls from parents who got a hundred phone calls from campers," said UG, wiping sweat from his wizened upper brow. He sat in an extra-wide director's chair, his name embroidered in calligraphic font across the back like he was Wes Anderson and not an asshole camp director that looked like a contestant on *The Biggest Loser.* He wore a navy blue visor and rubber slip-on sandals. Coarse black hair sprouted from his big toes like porcupine quills.

"I thought campers weren't allowed to use their cell phones," Dev said. "That they were just for emergencies."

UG shot him a cockeyed glance, his oval eyes flickering. "It's hard to police all the cell phones coming into camp," he said. "But that's really not the point. We have strict rules about counselors showing public affection in front of campers. It's just not appropriate."

"So, if we were campers kissing then it wouldn't a big deal?"

"Again, that's really not the point," UG got up from his chair and began to pace the room. "I have a camp to run and campers to protect and I can't have parents bombarding me with threats to withdraw their kids because they are being exposed to promiscuous behavior."

Dev scoffed a little. "Kissing in public is promiscuous behavior?"

"It is in the minds of ten year-olds."

"There are ten year-olds at this camp probably already sleeping with one another," Dev said.

"After seeing you guys go at it like that I wouldn't be surprised."

"If you think we're the reason—" he took a deep breath. "Mushky and I aren't even sleeping with one another."

"Dev, stop it."

"I'm not naïve," said UG.

"So—what?" asked Dev. "You want us to stay away from one another? Is that what you're saying?"

Suddenly, a terrible fear shot through me. Dev and I were going to be torn apart. We were going to get fired. Just when I was starting to actually like this awful place. I'd be exiled on a cheap charter flight with unassigned seating and snacks for purchase back to Boston. All the cool summer jobs snatched up long beforehand, I'd find minimum wage work at The Upper Crust on Newbury Street, serving pizza to wealthy South American students studying English at B.U. for the summer pretending to be poor because they thought it was way cooler than being rich, splitting any tips I got ten different ways with all the other behind-the-counter people, while Barrie sunned herself on a Thai beach oblivious to all the heartache and pain that she had triggered into action. And all because I French kissed a hot Irish Catholic boy with wavy blonde hair and a bra on his car.

Somewhere up in heaven my Russian-Jewish grandmother was cackling like the Three Witches in Macbeth: *Hahahahahaha!!!*

Dev would get canned as well. Broke, nothing but a stack of student loans and a half-tank of gas to his name, he'd spent the rest of the summer at home with his ailing mother with the ugly housecoat and the Jesus figurines above her bed and no money for her knee operation. And all because he French kissed a Jewish girl with gnarly hair and a perfect score on her PSATs during a Fourth of July fireworks display.

At that moment all I wanted was to be at this camp. I wanted to eat its lousy food and swim in its algae-infested lake and hang with my spoiled campers that talked about fantasy-fucking Nick Jonas and wore teeny bikinis you could fit in a contact lens case.

"I'm sorry," I declared. "It will never happen again."

Dev nudged me in the side. "Don't apologize," he said. "We didn't do anything wrong."

"Look," said UG. "These kids look up to you. They trust you. They're going to do whatever you do. And, Dev, I know this sounds horrible, but it doesn't help matters that you're not—" He hesitated, shifting back on forth on his Adidas sandals, sighing a little because he knew just how truly horrible what he was going to say was going to sound.

"Jewish," Dev said.

UG nodded.

"So what you're saying," Dev said, folding his arms against his chest. "Is that if I were....*Jewish* then it wouldn't be a problem if we were making out?"

UG nodded again. Dev just stood there. The hypocrisy of it all was beyond epic. Camp Kippewanscot served pork fried rice for Sunday night dinner and ham sandwiches for lunch. And now I was being punished because my summer camp boyfriend was an Irish Catholic vegetarian? I had become Juliet Capuletowitz. And Dev was my McRomeo.

It made me want Dev even more.

12:45 P.M. Rest Hour

The relationship got serious.

Forced to keep our relationship under wraps, Dev and I resorted to secret rendezvous at night down by the lake where he'd slide off my bra; in the athletic shed behind the baseball diamond where he'd go to second base on me; and in the kitchen behind the pantry where we did Whip-its and raided the refrigerator marked KOSHER, gorging ourselves on potato knishes and Ba-Tempte half-sour pickles.

It didn't matter anymore that Dev wasn't Jewish. Or that he had a bra on his car. Or that his mother had Jesus figurines above her bed and wore a horrible-looking housecoat. Or that when he pronounced my middle name—"Maaaalka"—he sounded like a Scandinavian tourist. A wave of excitement coursed through me every time he dug his hand underneath my t-shirt and went to unhook my bra.

So what if I had to bribe my campers with copies of *Teen Cosmo* and *Teen People* that I bought at the Circle K on nights off to keep them from snitching on me whenever I sneaked out of the bunk? (Ro' never had to submit to such measures; she seemed to come and go as she pleased, leaving a trail of cigarette smoke in the wake of her designer Grecian sandals as she padded down to the lake.)

And then one night we didn't have to sneak around.

"Our first night off together," Dev said. "*Finally.*" We pulled into the parking lot of the Holiday Inn in Mt. Pocono. It was short and square with its signature aquamarine and orange signage. "Counselors night off. No annoying campers. No stupid camp directors. Just us. You and Me. Nobody can tell us what to do." He took

my hand and squeezed it.

We glided through the hotel's sliding glass doors. The lobby furniture was

orange and the shag carpeting was green. Perched on the wood-paneled check-in desk

was a plastic display case featuring an assortment of tourist pamphlets for the Pocono

Blues Festival and Claws 'N Paws Wild Animal Park. There was free coffee and free

continental breakfast and a TV room with six working channels. Dev slid his Emerson

Visa credit card across the counter, tapping his fingers on the counter ("God, I hope it

goes through," he said under his breath). The hotel check-in clerk handed him a

jangling set of scratched silver keys hanging from a clear plastic rectangle with the

words HOLIDAY INN etched in white.

"Are you nervous?" asked Dev.

"No," I lied.

We took the elevator five flights up. We passed an ice machine, a vending

machine, a cart of toiletries and a utilities closet propped open and mint green folded

towels on its shelves. We came to our room: 613. There were 613 Commandments in

the Torah. It was a sign. Dev kicked open the door.

"You know," he said. "We can take things slow. We don't have to do anything

that you're not ready to do. We can wait as long as you need."

I glanced across the queen-size bed with its quilted brown and burnt sienna

bedspread. We didn't have to do anything that I wasn't ready to do, but I was ready to

do things that I wanted.

"I'm not a virgin," I reminded him.

"I know," he said, drawing a hand across my cheek. "But, you know, you said your first time wasn't—"

"Seriously," I said. "It's OK."

"Yea?"

"Yea," I nodded. "It's OK. I *want* to. Just don't play any Feist music."

Dev was a college boy. He knew what he was doing. He drew the blinds closed and lowered me onto the bed. He knelt down in front of me. He took off his ZBT hat and placed it on the floor. He slid off my socks and my sneakers and my shorts and my underpants. I don't remember what color underpants I was wearing that day, or what color shorts, but I remember them lying on a heap on the floor. He firmly spread my legs apart and lowered his head between them. I felt slow rising waves in the lower half of my body and then a sharp rush of sadness. The room felt dark and cold, even though it was July and eighty-five degrees outside. Everything inside me went slack. I wanted to be held and not so naked.

"Are you OK?" Dev asked me.

"Uh-huh."

"Did that feel—?"

"Yes."

"Did you—?"

"I did," I said. I looked away. "I'd never, you know—"

"Really? You mean not with—"

I shook my head. "No," I said. "This was the first time with anyone."

"Wow," said Dev. He slipped into bed next to me and spread a cool sheet on top of us.

"We don't have to do anything else," he said, playing with the knots in my hair. "We can wait."

"No," I told him. "I want to. Not everything, not now, but…I want to make you happy."

He took his t-shirt off. And then his shorts. And then his underwear.

And there it was, in the palm of my hand. I shirked, tilted my head, unsure what to make of it. I examined it closely. I'd only slept with one boy so I wasn't exactly a sexpert, but there was something slightly off about Dev's private parts.

"It looks like a turtleneck," I told him.

"It's called foreskin," he said.

And then, just as I was about to lower my mouth on my first Gentile penis, Dev's iPhone rang.

"It's my mother," he groused, springing from the bed. He grabbed his phone and headed for the bathroom. "I'll be right back," he said and closed the door behind him. He was gone less than a minute, but in that minute a wedge of melancholy grew between the queen-sized bed with its bad floral bedding and the bathroom with Dev inside it. My phone hadn't rung since I got to camp. My parents hadn't even called when my cousin died, ringing the main camp line instead. I was alone, naked, on a bed in a lousy Holiday Inn hotel room.

Dev emerged from the bathroom. "I'm so sorry," he said, climbing back into bed. "She gets really, really needy. It's hard for her all on her own."

"That's OK," I said. "I understand." But I didn't.

"You are literally the coolest girl that I have ever met in my whole entire life."

"It's OK. Your mom needs you. I get it."

"No," he said, wrapping me up in his arms. "I'm not sure that you do get it."

"What am I not getting?"

He kissed me. Long, slow, soft, a forever and forever and forever kiss that would last long past summer: "That I think I'm falling in love with you."

—

Our campers sang about us at mealtime:

> *Mushky and Dev*
> *Sitting in a tree*
> *K-i-s-s-i-n-g*
> *First comes love*
> *Then comes marriage*
> *Then comes baby in the baby carriage!*

We became a joke in the annual camp counselor review. We were a more gossiped about couple than anybody in *Us Weekly* or *People*. Forbidden from touching in public, we exchanged winks, waves and smiles. Dev mouthed "I love you" across the dock during the all-camp Shabbat free swim. Samantha loaned me her red string bikini—"It'll look so awesome on you!"—and it fit too-tight and too-small in all the right places. I loved her for saying so, even if my ass was twice the size of hers. Dev whistled as I walked by. There was nothing that UG could do to stop us.

Reed, the Red Cross-certified sailing instructor—dubbed Guitar Guy because he sat under a tree during free period composing bad rhymes while strumming the three chords to the guitar that he knew—composed a special song tribute about us:

> Dev and Mushky, they are in love
> Dev and Mushky, a sign from up above
> That even if one is a city girl big-assed Jew
> And the other is an Irish lad from outside of Syracuse
> That love can conquer, yes it can
> At Kippewanscot summer caaaaaamp!

For the first time in a long time, I was happy. I was falling in love. I was skipping across camp in my scuffed-up sneakers and cut-offs. I canoed around the sun-dappled lake with Samantha and Erika during free period saying things like "I love camp!" and "I love being a counselor!" and "Camp Kippewanscot rules!" During snack period, Dev and I would meet up on the lawn outside the dining hall and suck on frozen Otter Pops while our campers encircled us aiming water guns at our faces chanting: "Mushy and Dev! Mushky and Dev!"

I wasn't worried about the SAT exam or college applications or padding my résumé with extra curricular activities that I hated for the sake of impressing the admissions committee at Yale. I didn't even care about religion anymore. Counselors were penning ridiculously bad songs about me and I thought it was the most awesome thing ever. Camp was awesome! Life was awesome!

Mushky has a boyfriend! Mushky has a boyfriend!

We took arts and crafts activities to a whole new level, painting push pots together in ceramics, MUSHKY and DEV etched in hard baked clay. We passed love

126

notes to one another during evening activity. We sat on the edge of the dock as our

campers disrobed during Swim Safety Day, dipping our feet in the thick, murky water

and naming our unborn children.

"Ophelia," I suggested.

"Nicholas," he said.

"Lolita."

"Philip."

"Andrew."

"Noël."

"Chaim."

"*Christian Mendelssohn.*"

"*Mendel McGillicudy.*"

And then one late night, long after Taps and tucking in my campers with

promises of Twizzlers and fake tattoos if they kept their mouth shut (Margot wanted a

skull & bones; Samantha, a puffy heart), a balmy summer breeze tickling the leaves and

the sound of soft lake ripples, I found myself on my back on a soft bed of moss wearing

only my underwear and Dev moving breathlessly on top of me.

"I want you," he moaned.

I reached up to grab the back of his neck and noticed that it was smooth where

before my hand had pressed against a silver chain that left circular indentations in the

fleshy part of my palm.

"What happened to your Claddaugh necklace?" I asked him.

"It fell off," he told me. "It must be a premonition."

"Of what?" I asked nervously.

"I don't know. That maybe I'll light Chanukah candles?"

Six sexiest words spoken by a Gentile boy as he lay naked on top of you.

"I want to *be* with you," he told me. "I'll bake a challah if that's what it takes."

"I'll wear red. And green. Together."

"I'll learn Hebrew."

"I'll learn to like sourdough bread. And mayonnaise."

"I'll make kugel. And really bad boiled chicken."

"I'll sing Latin hymns."

"I'll *convert*."

And just like that, on a bed of moss and the glint of moonlight on Dev's sweaty pale skin and Lake Kippewanscot lapping quietly at the shore, I let a Gentile boy inside of me.

—

We were inseparable. We spent each day counting down the hours until we could be together, clandestinely ensconced in our mossy spot down by the lake when our campers were asleep, shrouded by the thick shade of a lush, coniferous pine tree whose branches and leaves curved across our bodies.

"I love you," I told him. It was the first time I'd ever told anybody. *I love you. I love you. I love you.*

We'd been together a month. In camps terms this is not a marriage—it's an eternity. As a celebration of our life together, on our next day off, we drove to New York City.

We signed out of camp, rolled the top down on Dev's Camaro, and steered it across the gravelly, two-lane roads of central Pennsylvania and the dull, grey highways of northern New Jersey. Dev played a mix he titled TOP TWENTY-FIVE AMERICAN IDOL WINNERS B-SIDES and I didn't complain once. He kept a hand on the inside of my thigh during the entire drive down and pulled over to go down on me in the parking lot of a Toys R Us in Elizabeth. We inched our way through the congested, jam-packed tunnel of the George Washington Bridge and spilled out into the city.

"I'm so excited to be away with you," Dev said, parking the Camaro in the only lot we could find that cost less than $40 dollars a day. "We're in New York. Hours away from camp. Nobody can tell us what to do. Nobody can tell us that we can't touch one another."

"Or that we can't flirt."

"Or that we can't hold hands."

"Or that we can't kiss."

"Or that we can't *fuck*."

Strolling up and down the streets of New York, my head spun a little. Strolling through the Met, studying the collection of Monets in the Impressionist wing—"I painted this in class," Dev told me as we examined *Wheatstacks (End of Summer), 1890-91* — I had an urge to hide. When Dev grabbed me and kissed me in full view of the security guard, a collection of oils and Klimt's "The Kiss," my cheeks burned hot.

Standing on the baking hot asphalt on Wooster Street with the July sun on the back of

my neck and a Betsey Johnson display window in front of me, I tried hard to focus on

the fact that for weeks I'd been aching for a day like this. But now I felt weird and

awkward, as if everybody was staring at us. I didn't want our longings visible to the

world. Camp wasn't the real world. What if God saw us?

Sitting in a back corner booth at Katz's Delicatessen, I hid my face behind a

giant menu. I hadn't even told my parents about Dev. Right at that very moment they

were in Israel, sitting *shiva*[9] for my cousin Shelli, unaware that the daughter they sent

to Hebrew school three days a week for thirteen years was cuddling in a brown leather

booth with an Irish-Catholic hick from upstate New York sampling his inaugural bowl

of matzoh ball soup.

"Delicious!" he cried out.

And then Dev's iPhone rang. And I was getting pretty sick of his mother.

"Again?" I asked. "Can't it ever just be the *two* of us?"

Dev looked at me. His eyes were limp, haunted and sorrowful. "It's been this

way my whole life," he sighed.

"I'm sorry. I didn't mean—"

"No," he said. "You're right. You deserve all of my attention."

---

[9] Seven day period of mourning where everyone sits around eating pastries and fruit and cold cut platters

For the first time in weeks, Dev switched off his ringer. For the first time that day, I kissed him in front of everybody.

—

The Days Inn on 94th Street had a cramped lobby with faux marble floor, fake leather couches, a plastic plant and a smudged glass coffee table with stacks of tourist pamphlets and an ashtray filled with half-smoked cigarettes. A group of teenage German tourists blathering in German and perusing *The Rough Guide to New York City* were squatting atop their oversized backpacks with patches of international world flags.

Dev and I climbed the stairs to room #201 (non-smoking, shag carpeting, Internet rate of $69 dollars).

"I want you naked," Dev said to me, pulling me towards the bed.

He peeled off my shorts and my t-shirt and my underpants. He slipped off my sneakers and pressed his clothed body against mine.

"We're going to be together forever," he said.

"Really?" I asked.

"Really."

"And when we get out of camp we'll stay in hotels that don't have stained brown bedspreads?"

"I promise," he said.

"And there won't be any sneaking around."

"No. Everybody will know about us."

"And my parents?" I asked.

Dev propped himself on his elbow. "I'll tell them that I love you," he said, "and that religion doesn't matter. And if it matters that much to them then I'll become Jewish."

"You're serious?"

"I'm not going to lose you."

"But you can't just *become* Jewish," I said. "You have to study and take classes. It's a whole huge thing. I could never ask anybody to do that for me."

"You haven't asked."

"But I'm only seventeen."

"And I'm twenty. So what? I love you, Mushky. You're different from any other girl I've ever met. I really, really love you." He brushed his lips, tender and warm, against mine. "Don't you love me?"

He smiled at me, eyes petulant and soft. "I love you," I said.

And I did. Of course, I did. I was only seventeen.

—

The ride back to camp was long and hot. We didn't turn off into any Toys R Us parking lots, but Dev rubbed my knee as he drove while mouthing the words to Jordin Sparks' latest single. We stopped for lunch at a New Jersey Turnpike Burger

King where we made out in a back corner booth and feasted on fries and a giant Coke. We shared a straw, blowing bubbles in our soda, proclaiming our true love.

We arrived back at camp with five minutes to spare. UG was waiting for us by the sign-in board, his hirsute arms jammed angrily against his protruding thick stomach.

"I need to speak with you both," he said. "Immediately."

Dev let his hand drop where before it was holding mine. We followed UG into his office, a space that was unfortunately becoming quite familiar. "What is it?" Dev asked, squinting his cool blue eyes.

UG drew one of those bottomless breaths after which you know only bad news can follow. "I know what you both have been doing."

"Doing what?" Dev asked. "We had our day off. We're back on time."

"It's not what you're doing outside of camp," UG countered. "It's what you've been doing *at* camp."

Dev and I looked at one another.

"Sneaking out of your bunks," said UG. "Heading down to the lake. It's a small camp. People talk."

I was going to say something about Ro'—her padding out of the bunk late at night with her crinkled pack of cigarettes, the carcinogenic affects of nicotine, how compared to secret sex with condoms down by the lake, Ro's menthols were what UG ought to be outlawing, not young, verdant, interfaith love. But I knew that it wouldn't matter. UG didn't give a shit about who smoked at camp. The Swedes smoked, the

Brits smoked. If he kicked out everyone with a pack-a-day habit he'd be left with the

nothing but a staff of C.I.T's, and half of them smoked, too.

"I'm docking you a day's pay," UG announced, rubbing the bridge of his

unevenly suntanned nose where a strip of SPF had been carelessly smeared. "You can

talk, obviously. You can spend time with one another—obviously *not* doing so would

be totally impossible. But if you don't stop, you know…" he circled his hands a few

times in the air… "*messing* around with one another on camp grounds, I'll be forced to

fire you *both*."

—

Something inside me snapped. As my campers slept, I whimpered into my

pillow. I thought about Shelli and how she was dead and down in the ground and how

her hair was still growing because I'd heard that's what happens. UG yelled at me again

and again in my head. *Fire you both. Fire you both.* I cried and cried, but Ro' didn't

hear me. She was smoking a butt on the steps of the bunk, flipping through the pages

of *Elle*, marking up model parts with a pen. My only consolation in this mess was that

she was more fucked up than I was.

I tiptoed over to Ruth's bed, careful not to wake her. I quietly opened the top

drawer to her cardboard Target dresser and drew out the box of purple stationery

upon which she'd scrawled tear-stained letters home to her parents. I helped myself to

a LOVE stamp and a pink colored pencil and sat on my bed. Using the copy of

Middlemarch I'd only read five pages of as a writing desk, I penned the following:

Dear Berkowitz,

I hate you. I fucking hate hate <u>HATE</u> you. For the past year I kept away from love because I knew that someday you and I would get married and I just didn't see the point. And now I've gone ahead and fallen in love with someone. And he's a goy. And blonde. And he drives a Camaro. And I've gone and slept with him. We have sex—at the Days Inn. On bad bedding. I'm ruined. And now I might get fired. And it's all <u>your</u> fault. Please write back. I miss you miss you miss you.

Love,
Mushky

    I slid the letter in an envelope, slid the envelope in a manila folder marked

OUTGOING MAIL. And waited to see what happened.

2:00 P.M. Fourth Period

Everything changed.

For the next several nights, instead of spending them with me in our now not-so-secret spot down by the lake, Dev got stoned behind the arts and crafts shack with a group of red neck counselors from Texas. Trent was a freshman at Texas A & M studying to become a landscape architect. He wore skintight biker shorts and ribbed tank tops everyday but swore that he had a girlfriend. He'd been dating her for the past six years, he told everyone, ever since their junior high school cotillion where he wore a Dolce & Gabbana tuxedo that he was stoked to find in a designer clothing resale shop in Dallas. I'm not sure he got that this proved he was gay and not that he wasn't. In any case, they planned to marry in a lavish Baptist ceremony on his uncle's dude ranch in Midland right after graduation. He gave the thumbs-up sign a lot and said "Howdy" whenever anyone walked past even if he didn't know the person's name.

Trevor, Trent's best friend from home, never smiled and moped around with his eyes half-closed like this whole camp experience was literally putting him to sleep. He wore jeans even when it was 90-degrees outside and had an unkempt mane of long brown hair that he kept pulled back in a black leather hair lacer.

"Hey." Dev coolly waved to me I passed by one night following evening activity. Rivulets of red ran through the whites of his bloodshot eyes, the blue in them now a dusky muted grey.

"What are you doing?" I asked.

"Nothing," he said. "Just hanging with my buddies Trent and Trevor." He slung an arm around each of the Texans in a way to suggest that he didn't know which was which.

"Oh." My heart sank.

"OK," he said, turning away as though we'd only just met, as though we were total strangers. "See ya later."

Free period, he didn't speak to me at all. He didn't flirt with me during snack. Or whistle as I traversed the dock in Samantha's red bikini that I'd officially traded for a pair of vintage Levi's with rainbow patches on the back pocket I'd scored from a dollar-bin at a thrift store in Harvard Square.

He spent a lot of time, alone, down by the dock. He was either making phone calls or taking phone calls, holding hand-cupped conversations to make sure that nobody could hear what he was saying. Was it his mother? It didn't even matter. Whoever it was, she was more important than me. He loved me, he told me, he loved me. But now I was invisible.

During the English version of the Kiddush at Friday night dinner—"Thanks, God, for the booze"—Dev didn't stand next to me and sip the watered-down Manischewitz from my paper cup like he used to. During lunch one day I caught him tousling the waist-length auburn hair of a pretty fourteen year-old C.I.T with legs as long as summer vacation. And when I went to visit him in the computer shack he pretended to actually care about his job.

"I can't talk right now," he told me, staring down at his keyboard.

"Can we talk later?" I asked. "After dinner or during evening activity?"

"I'm really behind on this computer program," he said. "These graphics are pretty complicated."

"It's not school," I said. "Suddenly you give a shit about your elective specialty?"

He stared at me hard. "Mushky," he said, "This is my *job*."

"Are you mad at me?" I asked, hating myself for sounding like exactly who I was— a vulnerable and confused seventeen year-old pleading with her summer camp boyfriend to pay her more attention. "I saw you flirting with that C.I.T."

"What C.I.T?"

"I don't know her name. The girl with the long hair and the long legs who always walks around with a tennis racket."

"Victoria? She's fourteen years old."

"So? I'm only seventeen."

"Mushky, you're being ridiculous."

"Then why are you ignoring me?"

"*Mushky*," he said, emphasizing my name but not in his usual good way. "I'm not ignoring you. I just don't want either of us to get fired. I can't afford to lose this job. As dumb as it is, I need that end-of-camp paycheck to help pay for my mother's operation."

"It's always about your mother," I grumbled. "Your mother's on the *phone*. Your mother needs your *attention*. That's a Jewish boy neurosis, Dev. You haven't converted yet."

For the first time in days, Dev cracked a smile, his mouth a flash of bright white. But his eyes were snake-like, steely and cold. He peered around the room at his campers, too consumed with video games to pay us much attention. Once the PDA of two sexually active camp counselors cooled off, the campers seemed to have no use for us. Campers didn't care about wilting relationships, only those in full flourish. There weren't a lot of camp break-up songs about relationships in crisis:

> They slept together down by the lake
> They got in trouble by the camp director
> Dev got baked.
> Now he's acting like Mushky doesn't exist
> Yeah, Camp Kippewanscot!

The words didn't exactly rhyme.

"Everything is going to be fine," Dev assured. "I'm just creating a little distance between us so that UG will leave us alone. Once things settle down, we're going to be together. I promise."

And I believed him. Of course, I did. I was only seventeen.

—

Visiting day and for some reason I missed my brother Bucky something awful.

Dev and I were on the back deck of the dining hall passing out Popsicles and Push-Ups. It was Janice's idea, putting us on snack-time patrol, and if UG had a problem with it then he could blame it on her. She still felt pretty bad about my cousin Shelli dying and having been the one to break the news, so when I begged her not to put me on Parent Patrol—greeting parents, shaking their hands, directing them toward their kids' bunks—she gladly obliged. I divvied out assorted rainbow flavors and Dev handed out the sugar-free and all-fruit options to all the overweight and diabetic kids. Assigning me to snacks was the first real work Janice had done all summer.

But UG didn't have to worry anyway, because Dev and I barely said a word to one another. A week earlier Dev said he'd become a Jew for me. Now, he was distant and frigid, as icy cold as the frozen fruit bars, our romance melting away in the hot July sun like the raspberry and lime popsicles.

But at that moment I wasn't focusing on Dev. I was watching a camper and her family as they cut across the soccer field. The girl was Victoria, the one with the long legs and the tennis racket that Dev lusted over even though he wouldn't admit it. The boy looked a little like Bucky—a little shorter, a little younger, same round face and eyes. Probably her brother, though I hadn't seen him around camp, maybe visiting from another one. Their parents were both handsome and tall and wore Camp Kippewanscot souvenir t-shirts over their regular normal clothes.

I was aching to call Bucky. But he was at his gifted and talented summer science program at Johns Hopkins and they weren't allowed to use the phones because they had to concentrate on being gifted and talented. And cell phones called cancer, which they learned about in one of their gifted and talented science classes. I could have told Bucky about Dev. He'd think it were cool that I was sharing a secret with him from our parents, and if he threatened to squeal then I could threaten him back with telling them about the time he bought a pack of tampons and dipped them in red paint and

140

gloated to his friends that he'd scored them from a girlfriend who didn't actually exist. He was fourteen and probably wouldn't have cared if Dev was Jewish or Muslim or a Sadist. But now it didn't really matter because I wasn't even sure if there was anything left to tell.

"Dev," I said. "Are we not talking?"

He handed a Push-Up to a chubby camper whose elasticized waistband was sliding down her butt. He tugged on the brim off his ZBT baseball hat and adjusted its fit. "We're talking," he said. But then he didn't say anything.

"Isn't it funny?" I asked, trying to make small talk. "Seeing all these kids' parents? Kind of gives you an idea of what kind of adults they'll grow up to be."

"Funny," he agreed. "Or frightening."

Samantha's mom sashayed past the dining hall in dangly gold earrings and a tiny pink sundress, her implants about as subtle as hot air balloons. She held Samantha by the hand. Later, Samantha would show me the care package her mom gave her filled with all sorts of goodies: candy necklaces and candy rings, colorful muslin tunics, lacy bras and a pair of gold, kitten-heeled sandals. "Suri Cruise has the *same* ones," Samantha told the whole bunk.

Earlier in the day, Ruth's mom had dragged me aside. "Did she get her period yet?" she whispered into my ear, pushing a folded fifty-dollar tip into my hand like that would somehow push things along.

"No," I informed, feeling a bit sorry that I couldn't tell her otherwise. She seemed so excited by the prospect of Ruth bleeding.

"Has she had any cramping?"

"She hasn't mentioned anything."

"But she's got her emergency box of maxi-pads ready to go?"

"Yes," I assured her. "They're underneath her bed."

"Oh, good," she said. "I'm so happy that she's in good hands."

Margot's mother was a no-show, but her father and stepmother came to visit. Her father wore a pink seersucker jacket and white golf pants. Her stepmother sported a mass of magenta hair piled atop her head like fresh-spun cotton candy, a sparkly red hairpin in the shape of a butterfly fastened at the scalp. I could see why Margot hated them. My heart gave a little yank as she stood there in her black, knee-high Doc Martens, black eyeliner smudged across her lids, limply accepting a hug from a couple of complete and total strangers attempting to pass as her custodial parents.

"Your parents seem nice," I said to Margot, trying to be positive.

"They're horrible," she said. "And you know it."

"Yea? Really? You can tell that I think they're a little—"

"Obnoxious. Weird. Posers pretending to be parents when really they'd rather be golfing?"

"No, I'm sure they—"

She shook her head. "Trust me," she said. "They *don't*."

I liked Margot, I decided.

UG, of course, put on a convincing show, pretending to like everyone. He rolled around in his golf cart, waving to parents, pinching campers' cheeks, exclaiming

"Two of my *favorite* counselors!" to every staff member in his way. I was just glad that nobody's mother or father asked him to point out the girl caught screwing her Gentile boyhood in the soggy grass by the lake.

"Hey," Dev said to me as the ice cream line started to thin. "I have something to tell you."

"What is it?" I asked.

"It's kind of....*weird.*"

"Is it about your mother?"

"No," he shook his head. "It's nothing like that."

"You don't love me anymore?"

"No, it's—"

"What?"

"It's something that's been bothering me for a while."

"Is it about Jennifer?"

"Jennifer—what made you think of her?"

"Are you in love with her? Is that why you've been acting all weird to me?"

"No. God, no. *No.*"

"So what?" I said. "Just *tell* me."

He drew a heavy breath. "I killed a chicken," he blurted out.

I stared at him for quite some time. "A chicken," I repeated.

"It was during rush week —"

"They made you kill a chicken?"

"They made ten of us sleep naked in a bed with our hands tied to the bedpost while eating corn on the cob dipped in cow shit—"

"You killed a *chicken*?"

"It's terrible, I know—"

"You're kidding, right? You're just trying to make me hate you. So I'll leave you alone—"

"No. I'm not. I swear. I really killed a chicken."

"But you're a vegetarian."

"I know," he said. "I was stupid. I was drunk and wanted to fit in. I was only eighteen—"

"I'm seventeen —"

"You eat chicken."

"Kosher chicken. And I don't kill it. I don't slaughter it as part of some barbaric college fraternity hazing ritual."

"What's the difference?" he shot back. "It's still dead."

"I feel sick," I said, clutching my stomach.

He pointed to his baseball hat with the ZBT insignia. "You're the one who thought it was so cool that I was in ZBT," he said. "You think just because a fraternity is Jewish that means it doesn't make you kill chickens?"

"You're lying. You're trying to push me away."

"I'm not," he said. "It's true. I just needed to tell you. You can hate me if you want."

As I sat there picturing Dev hacking at a hen's neck with a knife, a sharp cramp settled in my lower back. I did the math in my head. My period was due, but this wasn't my period—this was Dev-killed-a-chicken sickness. How could I ever trust someone that killed a live bird?

"I'm not a horrible person," he said. "I swear. It was a horrible thing to do. That's why I didn't want to tell you. I've been sick about it for months." He swallowed hard. "Why do you think I became a vegetarian?"

"But you.... *murdered* a chicken."

"I'm not perfect," he said. "But I do love you. And now that I've told you all this you probably don't want to be with me anyway."

"You're the one that's been acting so mean—"

"I love you," he said again. He tore open a Popsicle and licked it. "I love that you're mad at me for killing a chicken. And I hate not being able to kiss you. That's why I've been such a jerk, why I've been hanging out with Trent and Trevor and getting stoned and ignoring you and hitting on the fourteen-year-old tennis prodigy."

"She's a tennis prodigy?"

"Because I'm angry," he said, "And I'm frustrated. And I want to kiss you so badly right now, in front of UG, in front of everybody." He took a bite of his Popsicle, crushing it in his teeth. "I want to fuck you so badly right now that I swear it's going to kill me."

—

The very next day I got a letter from Berkowitz. Aside of one postcard from

my parents—"Beautiful Weather. Funeral sad. <u>So</u> sad. Weather amazing. Miss you. Love you,

Mom and Dad"—it was my first piece of real mail that summer. My heart pounded a

little as I pried open the envelope.

Dear Mushky,

I'm glad that you have found true love, even if he is a goy. Mushky, I miss you. Part of me wishes that I'd acted sooner on my feelings because now it's obviously too late. Hopefully, we can see one another soon, even if it's just as friends who said they'd get married if nobody else came along. I hate this summer job working at the bakery. I threw a banana muffin at my boss the other day. Anyway, I'll be on Long Island first week of August visiting cousins. Can you steal away from camp and meet me for a day in the city?

Love,
Berkowitz

I folded the letter, slipped it in the back pocket of my shorts, and ran to find

Dev. It was rest hour. He was shirtless, sunning himself on the far end of the dock. Ro'

was there, too, in a yellow one-piece with a cutout in the shape of a heart and

sunglasses as big as her head. A couple of the Swedes—Katerina and Helena—lay on

their stomachs in bikini bottoms and no tops, their hair swept up over their heads,

both of them hoping that UG would walk by and freak out that they were sunbathing

half-naked so they could make fun of him in Swedish.

"Dev," I said, hovering above him. "Are we spending our next day off

together?"

He looked up at me. "Don't you want to?"

"I do," I squatted down beside him. "I thought maybe we could go visit your mother?"

Dev whisked off his sunglasses. "You're kidding," he said.

"She's only a few hours away."

"Mushky, I don't bring anybody home to meet my mom."

"What about Sinead?" I asked.

Dev screwed up his face. "Sinead? We dated for seven years. She lived down the street. Her dad walked out on her, her mom was nuts and her house was a shit hole."

"My family's nuts."

"My mom sleeps with Jesus above her bed."

"You're the one that keeps talking about us being together, about telling my parents, about you converting—"

"Mushky, she's got a Jesus in the kitchen. In the bathroom. In her closet. In the garage. In the laundry room. The woman is obsessed."

"So what are you saying?" I asked. "That you can't bring me home because I'm *Jewish*?"

I thought about the silver Shabbat candlesticks in our living room at home, the pair that my great-grandmother had smuggled out of Russia while outrunning the pogroms. And then the framed bat mitzvah picture of me with a wavy mullet cut that was meant to be a straight blow-dry. And my report card from Hebrew School—all E's for Excellent—tacked up on the corkboard above the refrigerator. There were too many crucifixes and candlesticks in this summer camp romance. Dev and I were doomed.

"Mushky," said Dev. "Why are you crying?"

I hadn't noticed that I was. Ro' looked over, and the Swedes. Dev scanned the area on the lookout for UG. The coast was clear. He put his hand on mine, like he used to. "What is it?" he asked again.

"Dev," I quivered, resting my head on his shoulder. "I'm two days late for my period."

3:00 P.M. Fifth Period

Color War broke out.

It was Red Team versus Blue Team and Dev and I were on competing sides. Dev was recruited to paint posters; I was picked to pen team fight songs, although I didn't quite understand what my expertise was in the area. Then again, I'd been hired to head a radio broadcasting specialty and the only thing I knew how to do was press PLAY, REWIND and FORWARD on my iPod, a skill I suddenly wished I could apply to my own life. Play. Rewind. Forward.

The campers enrolled in my pathetic elective—at least they now knew who Bob Dylan was—covered the events of the week-long, camp-wide athletic competition on WKIP, Camp Kippewanscot's very first radio station. UG couldn't figure out how to rig a camp-wide radio system, so every day during fifth and sixth periods, my campers roamed around gathering updates and sound bites on everything from potato sack races to baton relays. They'd report back to the radio shack where they'd holler their findings into a megaphone that was hooked up to an antiquated speaker system (relic from the 1980's) that spit static across the camp. They'd report team scores, team upsets, and what manipulative evil schemes team captains were secretly hatching to sabotage the other team's chances of winning.

The big joke of the whole thing was that each year during a camp-wide closing ceremony, UG would announce that the winner was a "tie." Rumor was that he did this so as not to upset any campers that might pull their applications for the following

season because they were spoiled brats that couldn't handle losing.

But it's pretty damn difficult to focus on apache relays and obstacle courses

when you're seventeen and pregnant with your Irish Catholic summer camp

boyfriend's baby.

Why oh why did I have to be on red team? Five days straight, forced to wear the

color red. Red shorts. Red t-shirt. Red bikini that I would soon balloon out of once I

started to show. Red. Blood red. Period red. It was a cruel cosmic joke that UG—whom

in a fit of paranoia I presumed knew that I was knocked up—had orchestrated to

mercilessly teach me a mean-spirited lesson: This is what happens to nice Jewish girl

counselors who screw the Irish Catholic head of computers. *Red! Red! Red!*

"My parents are going to kill me," I told Dev standing in the dinner line that

night. Teams sat by color. There were pitchers of red and blue punches and

complementary colored fruit—strawberries and blueberries, watermelon and plums—

on every table. *Red!*

"You're *not* pregnant," he dictated in a low whisper, leaning into his blue food

tray as if to emphasis the blue and not the red. "We used protection every *time.*"

But I'd watched enough MTV reality shows about teenage pregnancy to know

that condoms are never effective protection against blonde Irish Catholic boys.

I was three days late when I sat in the computer shack during rest hour surfing

the Internet, researching abortion clinics and adoption agencies in the Pocono

Mountain area. There was nothing to be found, just bait tackle shops, gas stations and 7-Eleven convenient stores.

I was four days late when Ruth woke me up in the middle of the night.

"I think I just got my…period." She wept softly into her hands. She stared shamefully at her feet and pointed to her underpants. She looked up at me, pleadingly, her eyes almost as big as her boobs. She was only eleven and I took her hand. They were soft and warm, comforting. I knelt on the floor beside her bed and fished around underneath it for her keepsake stash of maxi pads.

"We'll have to call your mother," I said, leading her into the bathroom. "She'll be happy, I think."

"OK," she said, sniffling.

"Do you know how to use them?" I asked.

"I think so," she whimpered, closing the stall door behind her. "I can't believe I just got my period."

"Yea," I said. "Well, at least *someone* did."

I was five days late when I confided in Ro'. Ruth had spent all afternoon chasing me around camp asking me if her maxi pad was leaking. I liked Ruth, but I wanted to scream at her. She had no idea how lucky she was to be bleeding, even if she was only eleven. Ro' was just as annoyed as I was. She had zero interest in counseling campers on their menstrual cycles ("Can't her mom buy her a fucking book?"). I followed her down to her lakeside smoking spot where she ripped open a fresh pack of menthols.

"Ro'," I said. "I might be pregnant."

Unfazed, she handed me a cigarette. "You want?"

"Ro'," I said. "I might be *pregnant.*"

"Exactly. You must be so stressed. It's the perfect time for a cigarette."

"I don't smoke, Ro'. Even when I'm not pregnant, I don't smoke. I hold them sometimes but that's it."

She handed me one anyway.

"Just smoke it," Ro' prodded, elbowing me in the side. "It's not like you're actually going to have the thing."

"How do you know?" I said, angling the unlit cigarette at her.

"If you need help," she said, "you can use my father's obstetrical services free of charge."

"You want me to contact your father about getting an abortion?"

"It's not that big a deal. He'd done it for other friends."

"How many of your friends have had abortions?"

"Not that many." She tilted her chin upward and blew a ring of smoke into the air. "Two. Three."

"Well, what makes you think I want an abortion?"

"What are you Bristol Palin? You going to name the kid Twig or Stick or Trout? You're joking, right?"

I shrugged. "Maybe not," I said, twirling the cigarette around baton-style in my fingers. "Just because Dev is Catholic and in college and unemployed and calls his mother every time we have sex doesn't mean that he won't make a good father."

Ro' stared at me like I was crazy. She grabbed the un-smoked cigarette from my hand and stuffed it with a huff back in its pack. No use wasting a cigarette.

"You've lost it," she said, flicking the ashes from her cigarette into the lake. "My dad's got a private practice in Westchester. We can go there together on our next day off. Make a girls day of it if you want. Grab lunch and check out the mall afterwards. It's got a flagship Nordstrom. And I've got my mom's credit card. There's a huge Juicy Couture section."

To Ro' it all seemed perfectly logical, practical even. Why would any teenage girl in her right mind put herself through the trauma and hassle of having her summer camp boyfriend's illegitimate baby, face alienation from her family and friends, and sabotage her chances of getting into an Ivy League school, when she could instead spend the day shopping?

"I need to think about it," I told her.

"Suit yourself." She peeled her shorts and tanned legs off the rock's slick, mossy surface and hopped off onto the grass. "I'm here to help," she said, stamping out her butt with her sandal. "Seriously, I'm here for you. Just let me know if you change your mind."

—

Six days late for my period.

Dev and I were in the arts and crafts shack, way in the way back, behind an assortment of paint cans and tumblers of dirty brushes. We were sprawled out on a thick canvas that Dev had rolled out and stretched across the floor. His sweat fell like tiny droplets of paint on my skin as he rocked back and forth on top of me.

It was counselor's night and most of the staff had either gone bowling or to Buckeye. I told Ro' that I needed to stay behind and work on Color War songs — *Red team campers are reaching for a victory/Watch out blue team, just you wait and see—* and Dev was "working on posters." UG wasn't around—he'd flown to Boston to see a doctor about a second Lap Band surgery given his post-op weight gain. Dev locked the door and bolted it and played his *American Idol* mix so nobody could hear what was going on inside. Anyway, what did it matter if we got fired? I was pregnant with Dev's baby. We were playing with fire, but we didn't care if we got burned. Fire me. I'm pregnant! See what I care!

"I'm a little freaked out," Dev admitted, as we lay sated among the paints and brushes.

"Me, too," I said. "If I am pregnant—"

"Mushky, I was thinking—"

"What would we do?"

"Mushky, I know we're both really stressed out—"

"Maybe we should take a test?"

"Maybe we're overeating. Maybe you'll get your period."

"I'm never late. Never."

"Maybe we should wait. Just a few more days—"

"For what?" I asked. I was feeling dizzy, nauseated, lightheaded, my body pumped full of pregnancy progesterone.

"I don't know," Dev said, rolling off the canvas. "I'm not sure what we should do. Where do you get a pregnancy test around here? It's not like they sell them at the canteen along with M&M's and Hershey bars."

He grabbed his blue clothes and threw them on. "This is probably a dumb time to bring it up," he said, zipping up his shorts. "But I talked to my mother this morning."

"Right," I sulked. "Your mother. Your *real* girlfriend. She always comes first."

"She really wants me to come home this week. She's feeling lonely and depressed. This summer has been really hard on her. She really needs me to be there."

"I need you."

"She's my mother—"

"Right. Your mother. And I'm just the girl you got *pregnant*."

"She's desperate, Mushky. What do you want me to—"

"Whatever," I said, yanking my red tank top over my head and stepping into my red shorts. "I've got plans anyway."

"No you don't."

"Yes, I do. With Berkowitz. We're going to meet in New York for the day. We've got the whole thing planned."

"Sounds great," he said. "Maybe you can run off and get married."

"Maybe we will. By a *rabbi*."

"Just don't get on my case for going home to visit my mother when you're running around the city with the guy you're *really* in love with—"

"Leave me alone," I said, stomping across the arts and crafts shack, tripping over a can of paint.

"Fine," he said. "I will."

"Oh, yea? Well fuck *you*." And I slammed the art and crafts shack door.

—

Berkowitz had a change of plans.

"I can't make it to the city," he told me over the phone.

"No," I said. "Why not?"

"I'm just as pissed off as you are. I was going to take the train from Jericho but now my grandmother is planning this stupid family barbecue thing. I'll be stuck there all week with my weirdo cousin Stanley who just got back from a yeshiva in Israel and turned totally religious and doesn't touch girls anymore or watch TV. Personally, I think it's just a cover up because the guy is 27 and still can't get *laid*. Ever notice how Jewish people tend to get religious when they can't find anybody to be *not* religious with?"

"And you can't get out of it – even for a few hours?"

"I've been fighting with my parents about it all week. They keep giving me the guilt trip. They're like, 'But you haven't seen Stanley in a *year*. He's your first *cousin*. You guys are *family*.' They are so totally annoying. I can't wait 'til I go away to college and never have to talk to them."

I sighed. It was so good to hear from a guy who wanted nothing to do with his parents. "I'm so bummed I'm not going to see you."

"Me, too," he said. "It sucks. Really sucks. How are things going with Super Goy?"

"They're…" I'd never lied to Berkowitz before. "I don't know. It's hard to having a relationship at camp."

"How come you're not spending your day off with him?"

"Because, he's going to visit his…mother."

"You're kidding. Why would anybody want to do that?"

"I know, right?"

"Are you sure that he's not Jewish?"

"Berkowitz, I'm *sure*. He drives a Camaro with a bra and his mother goes to church every Sunday and he's a Fine Arts major and doesn't have a job lined up after college and he has really good hair."

"Definitely not Jewish."

"And he killed a chicken. During rush week."

"He killed a chicken? Like, with his bare hands?"

"And he likes Taylor Swift."

"You're kidding."

"He considers her a songwriting genius."

"Jesus, Mendelssohn, what the hell do you *see* in this guy?"

I saw Dev's fair blond hair. I heard the way he said my name. I felt my skin get warm every time he touched me. And the rain that first time we kissed, how wet we were, clinging to one another, raindrops catching in the crevice of my breasts, the rain falling harder and harder. I felt Dev's child swimming around in my stomach.

"There's no way you can make it to the city?" I begged Berkowitz. "I'd come to Long Island but by the time I'd get there I'd have to turn around and come back. "

"I know. I thought of that. Believe me, Mendelssohn. I've tried to get out of this a thousand times."

"It's OK." I sighed heavily. "But we'll see one another soon?"

"Definitely. I totally miss you. You're coming out to Cali for winter break, right? I'm supposed to get this sick surfboard so we can take it out on the waves. My family really wants to see you. They're being totally lame about this cousin Stanley thing but you know how much they love you—"

"That sounds great," I said. "Definitely. I really can't wait to see you."

"I miss you, Mendelssohn."

"I miss you too, Berkowitz."

I hung up the phone and bawled my eyes out.

—

I met my mother at the Krispy Kreme in Penn Station. She was tan from her trip to Israel, dressed in white pants and a white shirt to show off her shimmery summertime glow. She flew swiftly through the station, like a soaring seagull, her arms stretched outward for the impending hug. Waiting for her, I had already eaten two original glazed and a coconut donut. I wasn't sure if this was a pregnancy craving or just nerves.

I was seven days late.

"You look amazing!" squealed my mother. "I am so happy to see you!"

My boobs had grown bigger. Did my mother notice? Had I imagined it? Could that happen on a two-hour Greyhound bus ride from Mount Pocono to Penn Station? Had the heat made them swell? She didn't exclaim how skinny I looked, which she did even during my fat stage when I was twelve. This made me very, very nervous. Did I look pregnant already?

We made our way to the taxi dispatch and my mom whipped out a photo album filled with snapshots from Israel. There were dozens of my cousins. And one of my mother wearing a doily on her head, pressing her forehead against the Western Wall[10] in one of those requisite postcard prayer shots. And then, oddly, a snapshot of Jon Voight with his arm slung around my father.

"That's Angelina Jolie's father," said my mother.

---

[10] Last remaining wall of the Second Temple in Jerusalem. The Romans razed it to the ground in 70 BCE. Think the biggest synagogue you've ever seen, but where Jews used to sacrifice lambs and rams and stuff. But not chickens.

"Mom, I know who it is. He's on all those Chabad telethons dancing around with the Hassids trying to raise money."

"He's a very good friend to Israel."

"Mom, he's a weirdo right-wing Republican." I wasn't the most knowledgeable teenager in the world when it came to politics, but I knew that if you shopped at Urban Outfitters and read books that were banned in foreign countries than you were a Democrat. If you wore knee-length skirts and bows in your hair and read books without swear words, then you were a Republican.

"He's a huge movie star," said my mother. "He won an Oscar."

"He was huge, mom. Now he grants interviews to *Us Weekly*. Angelina barely speaks to him."

"No, they're talking again. He told us. He and your father had a lot to talk about. They really hit it off."

"That's seriously disturbing." My mom was talking about my cousin Shelli's funeral like it was a week on a Carnival cruise ship. "How are Shelli's parents?"

"Devastated, obviously. God help them, I have no idea how they're going to get through this. The whole thing is just so tragic. But he was such a nice guy," she said. "And *such* a good friend to Israel."

My mother had this incredibly irritating habit of repeating the same sentences over and over again. I'd often wondered if this was a sign of Alzheimer's or just a nervous tic, as I'd heard similar complaints from Barrie about her own mother.

As our Pakistani taxi driver wound our way through the heavy midday traffic, I had a sinking feeling that my mom was never going to shut up about Jon Voight, like when my Great Aunt Judy met Madonna in the Montreal airport and said that she invited her to a celebrity Simchat Torah dinner. I was pregnant. I didn't give a shit about Jon Voight.

As our taxi inched across Midtown, I began to get a prickly feeling on my skin, like a ghost was trailing me. I saw Dev everywhere.

I saw him on the steps of the Met, climbing its stairs en route to the Monet exhibit. And by a hot dog stand that we'd strolled past, the vendor brandishing a pair of locking tongs, a limp knockwurst in a death grip. I saw Dev outside a Duane Reade where I considered stopping in for pregnancy test (How would I sneak it past my mom?). I saw him on the corner of West 34th and Broadway as our taxi pulled up to the curb. "Let's check out the back-to-school sales," My mother breezily suggested as she headed into Macy's.

We blew through main floor Cosmetics where I imagined him waiting for me by the Clinique counter (It was bonus time). I saw him by the Mac counter. I saw him so clearly that I was sure my mother could see him too. I felt certain that she was going to confront me: *Are you pregnant with your goyfriend's baby?*

She didn't, of course. Instead, she made a beeline for Home Goods and proposed I browse the Junior's department. I was relieved that she'd suggested a separation. I wanted to be as far away from my mother and her Jon Voight obsession as humanly possible. I couldn't understand how Dev could volunteer to spend so much time with his own mother.

I hopped on the escalator, ascending toward everything snug-fitting and studded. I wandered the various labeled sections of brand names, winding my way through racks of terry cloth and velour, running my hand along folded piles of designer sweat suits, designer jeans, and designer shoes in varying degrees of pastels. I tossed a few sweatsuits across my arm, hauled them into the dressing room and locked the door behind me.

I stood in front of the three-way mirror, stepped into a melon-colored puff-sleeved sweat suit, and struck a deal with God. *God*, I said, *if You make me not pregnant, then I will never sleep with a Gentile boy again.* No, wait. That was racist. *God, if You make me not pregnant, I will never sleep with any boy. Ever. Period.*

I looked ridiculous in the sweatsuit. If I had gone with Ro' to her dad's to get an abortion, this is what she would have made me buy. She would have added giant diamond hoops like from a hip hop video, paired them with spiked heels and dragged me to get my nails done in Gisele's favorite shade of pink (OPI Bubble bath).

I slid off the sweatsuit. Standing in my bra and underwear, I examined my figure closely. I hadn't gained weight at all. If anything, I'd lost a few pounds, flat where residual baby fat used to be. Ro' would be proud, but I wasn't all that surprised. Over the course of camp, I'd caught Kashrut Fatigue, laziness in keeping kosher. It was a common condition in observant Jewish kids at camps all over the country with optional kosher meal plans, or so I'd heard. Ringing the bell every time I wanted a hamburger that had been ritually slaughtered and rabbinically blessed had become such a nuisance that I basically just picked at salads and veggies, chasing it all down with diluted fruit punch that tasted like Robitussin cough syrup.

Staring at my skinny figure I had visual confirmation: There was no way that I was pregnant. God loved me. God was listening.

I tossed the sweatsuits aside and went to find my mother.

We left Macys empty-handed and hailed another cab to a little Israeli restaurant on the Upper West Side that according to Zagat's served the best hummus outside of Tel Aviv. My mother showed me more snapshots of my father and Jon Voight: "Such a *good* friend of Israel."

I didn't mention Dev at all.

But then my mother dipped a pita slice in a plate of garlic hummus and my pregnancy panic returned.

"There's some local neighborhood gossip," said my mother.

"Oh, yea?"

"Aaron Epstein had a baby."

I nearly choked on my falafel ball. "Aaron Epstein? Aaron Epstein from the grade below me in Hebrew school? Aaron Epstein with the zits all over his face?"

"Aaron Epstein," confirmed my mother.

"Aaron Epstein got a girl pregnant? He's skinny and ugly. Nobody wanted to date Aaron Epstein."

"His parents tried to keep it private. But, you know, you can only keep that sort of thing secret for so long."

I pressed my hand against my concave stomach, willing it to stay that way. "Are you sure—Aaron Epstein had *sex* with someone?"

"That's exactly what your father said. Can you believe it? He used to race around the synagogue playground with snot all over his face during High Holiday services."

"Who's the girl?" I asked.

"Not Jewish," she said, rolling her eyes. "Her name is Carla DeMatteo or Katie De Mattia or Kristin DeMotta—something like that. She's fifteen-years-old and from Billerica." My mother peered around the restaurant and cupped her hand over her mouth. "They're raising the baby *Catholic*," she hoarsely whispered. "They're going to *baptize* it. Aaron's mother is *beyond*. Did you know her father was a Holocaust survivor? Her older brother is a rabbi—in Ukraine, no less. Saving the remaining Jewish community. Her father's not talking to Aaron, Aaron's not talking to him. He's threatening to never let his parents see the baby. It's a mess. She's undone about the whole situation."

My mother dabbed her mouth with a napkin. "Thank God I don't have to deal with that with either you or your brother," she said, waving down our waiter for the check. "You should only marry someone Jewish. Trust me—otherwise it will be a complete *disaster*."

4:00 P.M. Free Period

Eight days late.

Eight days of Chanukah. Eight days no period. I was hoping for a miracle. Dev picked me up at the Poconos bus station. We drove back to camp with the Camaro top down, his wheat-colored hair fluttering as a hot wind whipped through it. My hair was dry, the ends all split from not having cut it in two months. We were listening to a just-released Adam Lambert single and didn't say much until Dev jerked the car to the right and pulled over on the side of the road. He grabbed me and kissed me hard.

"I'm so sorry," he said. "I missed you. I had the worst time ever at home."

"What happened?" I asked.

"Nothing," he said. "That's the thing. Everything was the same. The Jesuses on the wall. The TV from fifteen years ago. The ugly gingham plaid tablecloth with the cigarette burn. It made me realize something."

"What?"

"That if I ever have to go home to that place, I'll seriously lose my mind."

"You won't go home," I told him. "You'll stay in Boston. You'll get a really great job. Maybe you'll move to New York. Or Europe—"

"Mushky," he said. "Do you have any idea how competitive it is out there? How many jobs do you think are out there for college grads with degrees in painting?"

"Graphic designers. Web designers. Jobs in creative advertising—"

"But I don't know if I want to *do* any of those things." He tapped the black vinyl steering wheel in profound thought. "Sometimes I think all I might want to do is move to the woods somewhere and paint."

I ran my fingers through his soft, corn-silken hair. "You'll figure it out," I told him.

"But what if I don't?" He pushed away my hand. "Do you know how much money I'm going to owe in student loans? Eighty-thousand dollars. I'm so completely stressed."

"I know," I said. "But I'm stressed, too."

He looked at me. "Nothing?"

"Nothing," I said. "I've been telling you for days. We need to get a pregnancy test. I'm eight days late. I'm never late. Ever."

In five more minutes we were due back at camp. "Is there a pharmacy around her?" he asked. "UG is going to kill us if we don't make sign-in."

"Fuck UG," I said. "My parents are going to kill me. Nobody gets pregnant in my family unless they're married and so sick of one another that they already want a divorce."

"We'll get a test. Tomorrow. There've got to sell them somewhere. People must have unwanted pregnancies around here."

"It's your birthday tomorrow," I reminded him. I'd been remembering it all summer, since the moment he first told me.

"So?"

"Do you want to find out that I'm pregnant on your birthday?"

"You're not pregnant. You're not. You can't be, OK? We'll confirm it with a test and then celebrate with a round of drinks at Buckeye."

"But what if I am—?"

"You're stressed. That's all."

"Well, then how come all the other times in my life that I've been stressed my period didn't disappear then?"

Dev swallowed hard. He looked at his watch. "We've got to get back," he said. "It's ten. We're late."

"I know," I sighed impatiently. "That's what I've been telling you."

—

The morning of Dev's birthday, I found him in the arts and crafts shack, surrounded by cans of paint and brushes and buckets of dirty water. His t-shirt was splattered with reds, blues and yellows. There was paint on his face and his hands and his hair. Bars of morning sunlight beamed through the windows, falling across Dev's thick golden hair, backlighting it in such a way that it looked like a Jesus-like halo was perched atop his head.

Dev flicked his brush across a huge, cream-colored canvas. Thousands of tiny multi-colored dots configured in a pattern to form a foreboding image of a judge cloaked in black, brandishing a gavel overhead and the slogan in ominous all-caps: JUDGEMENT DAY COLOR WAR SONG FEST CAMP KIPPEWANSCOT 2010

A Kelly Clarkson song was playing on Dev's iPod and by this time I knew all the words. And liked it. Her songs now had meaning to me. *My life would suck without you...*

I shut the door and locked and bolted it behind me. I tiptoed toward Dev, gripping a crinkled brown bag behind my back. "That poster is amazing," I told him.

"I hope so. I spent more time on this stupid thing than on my final semester art project." He studied his work with a long, squinty glance.

"Happy birthday," I said. I held out the bag. "Your birthday present."

He slipped the paintbrush he'd been using in his back pocket, took the bag from me and pried it open. He reached inside and pulled out the ceramic artist palette that I had made him. It was sloppy, lopsided, thicker on one side than the other, and the thumb holder was way too wide. I made it during the rainy period, along with all the push pots, when I didn't know what was going to happen or if anything was going to happen, but I knew even then that I wanted him to remember me. My name MUSHKY MALKA MENDELSSOHN was engraved on the back.

"Do you like it?" I asked. "I figured you can take it back to school and use it when you paint."

"I love it," he said. He turned it over and saw my name. "It's the nicest birthday gift that I think I've ever gotten."

"Honestly?"

"Honestly."

"Maybe you'll use it to paint something that sells for millions of dollars and hangs in the Met."

He went to hook his thumb around the palette and it slid halfway down his arm. We both laughed. "If I ever paint anything worth selling," he joked, "it will definitely be because of this palette."

He placed the palette on the floor. "I'm lost," he said glumly. "I have no idea what I'm doing with my life."

"I'm scared," I said. "I'm really, really scared."

"I'm scared, too."

"I love you, Dev."

"Oh, Sunshine," he said. "You're too good for me."

And we did it right there, up against the arts and crafts shack wall, not bothering to take off our red and blue t-shirts. I got paint on my hair and on my face and on my thighs. Dev's paint-smeared fingers feverishly explored places on my body where no boy—Jewish or Gentile—had ever gone. He knelt in front of his poster, his right foot catching on an area of canvas that would later need to be retouched. I knelt down too and took his penis and its foreskin turtleneck in my mouth. Then we both slid to the floor, our arms and legs tangled up in one another, and Dev held me there for a long time, ignoring the camp-wide bell that echoed across camp, signaling the end of breakfast and the beginning of clean-up.

"You never drew me," I said to him, studying his poster. "Remember, you said that you would? Right when we first met?"

"I will," Dev told me. "I promise. Once we get out of here I'm going to do everything for you."

But as he kissed my forehead, I knew that he never would. But it felt good to believe him, bathed in the warm sunlight, him kissing me all over, and I didn't say a word.

I was nine days late for my period.

—

It was a tie.

The Color War Song Fest lasted two long hours. The rec hall was packed, stuffy and airless, like one of those Native American sweat tents in which tourists traveling with weirdo spirituality groups get asphyxiated and die. Dev's blow-job-poster earned top place honors, eliciting a spirited round of applause from both red and blue teams. Counselors presented camper awards of the Most Enthusiastic and Most Improved and Most Awards variety. There were counselor "comedy" skits that left me feeling embarrassed for those performing them. And there was a lot of clapping and cheering and singing, all of it off key and out of tune.

Blue team's fight song was to the tune of a *High School Musical* number that, despite my summer camp education in the way of Vanessa Hudgens nude Internet photos and Zac Efron gay rumors, I still didn't recognize.

> *Blue team campers*
> *Are chasing down a win*
> *Head of Waterfront*

Loves to go and swim
Blue team win (3x)!

I glanced around the rec hall, picking my campers out in the crowd. We'd spent nearly two months together, and they'd grown on me, but I was feeling a little sad at how little we had in common. It wasn't just that they were six years younger than I was, they were new and fresh and pure and untouched. They talked about sex a lot, but only in vague, amorphous terms. They talked about wanting to take Taylor Lautner's clothes off, but they didn't really know what that meant. They had no idea what sex really was, or the Gentile foreskin that accompanied it. None of them had given an Irish boy a blowjob, not that I knew of anyway. By the time they did give blowjobs and surrendered their virginity to insipid, self-absorbed child actors and took up with goys that killed chickens, they probably wouldn't even remember me. I wanted them, too, hoped that they would, but I had a feeling that after this summer, I was going to be obsolete.

I was never really a part of this mafia camp family.

I watched Erika. She was standing around in a circle with fellow blue team members, jumping and cheering and flailing her arms and clapping. Her hair was in a whale spout ponytail, a tomato-red hair bow twisted around it. I walked over and joined in. She saw me dancing and stopped clapping, her mouth aghast. "What are you doing?" she asked.

"I can't sit here?"

"You're on blue team."

"It's not Apartheid."

"Apart—what?"

"Color war is over."

"It's not over. They haven't announced the winner yet."

"I know," I said, "but I was thinking. Maybe you could teach me some of those *High School Musical* songs before the end of the summer."

"I thought you didn't like that movie. You said you watched it, but I'm not stupid. I know you didn't. I know you watch boring channels like CNN and Fox."

It occurred to me just then how badly I wanted my campers to like me. "I don't watch Fox," I said. "Fox is for Republicans."

She placed her hands on her hips. "You don't watch movies with singing and dancing."

"Is that bad?" I asked.

"The movies you watch are boring."

"How do you know?"

"Is Robert Pattinson in them?"

"No, but I know who he is. And I don't think they're boring. You might not either when you get a little older."

She shook her head. "Adults like boring and sad movies," she said. "I don't ever want to be an adult if it means I've got to be boring and sad. Movies where people sing and dance are just more entertaining than ones where they just sit around talking like boring sad regular people."

I walked off sadly and left her to dance with her friends.

Back on the red side, I spotted Margot. She looked miserable in her red t-shirt and red shorts, sulking in the back row, not bothering to even mouth the words to camp cheers. Her iTunes was filled with songs about rage and unrequited love and wanting to kill your parents. I felt fairly certain that she'd never seen any of the *High School Musical*s even if she could pretend a little better than I could that she had. At one point during the evening, I caught her smiling at me and I wondered if she'd think it were totally weird if I asked if we could hang out after camp ended.

At long last, UG took the stage. He was dressed diplomatically, in blue shorts and a red t-shirt, blue hat and red socks, his trademark bullhorn in hand. Everyone screamed and shouted and banged the floor and the walls with their feet and hands. Campers chucked empty water bottles and spitballs across the room. They smacked one another. Boys twirled their t-shirts above their heads, showing off their smooth pre-pubescent chests. Girls lifted up their t-shirts just short of revealing their training bras and giggled in mock embarrassment. UG gazed at the crowd and raised his bullhorn in the air like he was about to plant the American flag on Mount Everest.

"Camp Kippewanscot," he shouted, "It's time to announce the winner of Color War!"

The banging grew thunderously loud. I just wanted it to be over so I could take off my stupid t-shirt and change into something that wasn't red.

"And it's a tie!" UG shouted.

And like that, the crowd fell to a hush. UG walked off-stage, rested his bullhorn at his side, and patted a scattered few staffers on their backs, pleased with himself that nobody was going to call home that night crying that they'd lost. Next year, they would all happily return for another eight thousand dollar summer.

—

Color War was over, it was Dev's twenty-first birthday and, for the first time all summer, the bouncer at Buckeye refused to let me in. I was stuck outside with Ro', in a violet sundress, purple lip gloss and a pair of Ro's silver Lanvin sandals, my forbidden entrance made all the more humiliating by the fact I'd let Ro' spend an hour doing my make-up.

"What do you mean she can't go in?" asked Ro'. He'd waved her inside but lowered his thick, hairy arm in front of me like a gated barrier in a parking garage.

"She doesn't have an I.D."

"Neither do I."

"It's not up to me," he said. "I can only let a certain number of kids in without I.D.s."

"But you've been letting us in all summer."

"You can go in. She can't."

"Well, we're not splitting up."

As Ro' begged fruitlessly for my entrance, I couldn't believe that this was me. I didn't want to be one of those whiny seventeen year-olds angling for admission into a bar that didn't even have a decent cue stick or toilet paper in its bathroom stalls. Last time I was there, I found dried fecal matter on the toilet seat. Now I wished that, months ago, despite my stupid idealistic moral misgivings, Barrie and I had gone to that basement apartment on Tremont Street where an undergraduate at Boston College sold lost and stolen drivers licenses.

"This is bullshit," Ro' told the bouncer.

"You can fight with me all you want," he told her. "She's not getting in. You can leave with her if you want."

"She's not pretty enough?" asked Ro'. "I spent an hour doing her make-up and blow-drying her hair."

The bouncer eyes me up and down. "Sorry, kid, but it's not my decision."

Ro' huffed and rolled her eyes. The day before she received a care package from her parents filled with boxes of various colored contact lenses (even though she had perfect 20/20 vision) from one of her father's ophthalmologist friends. Tonight she was in a color called Caribbean Green and when she looked at you she had an evil glint like maybe she was going to kill you and tape you up on her collage of supermodels. "I think they make me look a lot more like Gisele," she announced, standing in front of the mirror putting them in.

"Look," the bouncer told Ro'. "There's a been a rash of underage drinkers this summer and the police have been hanging out so the owner is really clamping down. Blame it on your camp director. He's the one who phoned the bar."

Of course it was UG. I should know known. He was going to do everything he could to keep Dev and I apart, up until the bitter end.

"It's her boyfriend's birthday," Ro' protested, pointing inside the bar. "He's inside. He's been waiting for her."

"If he's her boyfriend then why isn't he out here with her?" he asked.

Ro' shook her head. "It doesn't work that way. It's a summer camp thing."

In line behind us, a bunch of Swedes grew impatient, tapping their sandaled feet and mumbling a string of Swedish cuss words: "Förgrymmat också!" One of the girls, a brunette with a nose ring named Alma, wore a t-shirt stretched tight across her ample chest that read SWEDISH SLUT LOVES TO FUCK. The bouncer looked at his watch and yawned.

"There's a pizza join down the road," he said to me. "They have beer. They'll let you in."

"But she's not even *drinking*," Ro' protested. She leaned in close and whispered loudly enough so that everyone could hear. "She thinks she might be pregnant."

I stomped off in a rage. Ro' called after me but I kept on going. I knew that in her own screwed up way she meant well, but at that moment I wanted to grab her by the hair and fling her into the lake. *Mittleschmertz* be damned. When I didn't hear the clomp of her wooden sandals trailing me from behind I knew that she'd gone inside the bar, ordered a beer and was now sidling up to whatever slobbering townie would pay her attention and compliment her hair accessories.

I was shaking so badly as I wandered down the long dirt road back to camp, at first I didn't hear that somebody in the dark kept calling out my name.

"Mushky!" echoed the effeminate voice. "Hey, Mushky, is that you?"

As the voice got closer, I made out a wiry, tree-like figure with bony, branch-like arms and stem-like legs that ambled clumsily through the woods. It was Brian Bluestein.

"It's Brian. Brian Bluestein."

We hadn't said much to each other since the night of the welcome dance when I broke his heart and danced with Dev, but here he was now, smiling at me. As he moved toward me, I fidgeted with the yellow copper moon necklace that Dev had made me. I hadn't taken it off all summer, but now it felt heavy. The edges dug into my skin, and the frayed leather cord scratched my neck.

"Mushky," Brian repeated, doing a little wave. "Hey."

"Hi, Brian."

"I'm on my way to the bar. You headed that way?"

I gave a dismissive little shrug. "Just left. It wasn't that fun."

"No? You're not with that Dev guy?"

I didn't answer. "Hey, Brian," I said. "Do you know if there's a pharmacy anywhere around here?"

—

Brian drove me to an all-night pharmacy fifteen miles away from camp. The

inside of his brand new black Prius smelled like pine. We listened to an alternative

music station and when I asked if he'd watched *American Idol* he said he'd never seen

an episode because it interfered with the Tuesday night conversational Hebrew class

that he taught in the Harvard Extension program. He knew that the Jonas Brothers

were an all-boy band but had no idea they were Christians saving themselves for

marriage; he thought they were Jewish because of their last name. He had no idea who

Ashley Tisdale was. "I like 70's and 80's music," he said. "Old School stuff. Ever listen

to *Bruce Springsteen and the E Street Band Live: 1975-1985*? It's pretty amazing." Aside

of the circular bald patch on his head and the nerdy all-white sneakers, I should have

been madly, madly, madly in love. But I wasn't.

"What do you need to buy?" he asked as we pulled up the pharmacy.

I could have lied. I could have told him to wait in the car. I could have

pretended that Ashley/Ashland had begged me for the latest issue of *Teen People* with

Selena Gomez on the cover.

"I need to buy a pregnancy test," I told him straight out.

Brian didn't blink an eye, even the one that twitched. He followed me into the

pharmacy and strolled alongside me down the aisles. He didn't say much as we passed

neatly stocked boxes with cleverly inspired names all promising first responses and

clear and simple results and accuracy beyond error. It could have been weird, shopping

for home pregnancy tests with a guy you'd spoken to maybe twice all summer who drove you to a 24-hour pharmacy at ten-thirty at night when the boyfriend who got you into this mess in the first place was back at a dive bar pounding vodka shots to celebrate his 21st birthday. But the only weird thing about it was that it wasn't even that weird.

"I guess I'll take this one," I said, plucking a generic brand off the shelf. "It's on sale."

Brian was such a sweet guy that he even paid for it.

We drove back to camp listening to Bruce Springsteen songs like the whole event was no big deal. I liked Brian. Not in that way, but I liked him, maybe even wished I liked him more. I wondered what would happen if I asked him to stop the car and then leaned over and unzipped his dark wash jeans. I wished I wanted him. Wished. But wishing accomplishes nothing.

—

We got back to camp a little before midnight, well in time for curfew. The moon shone white in the sky, casting a milky-blue hue across the soccer field. Brian was a perfect gentleman, holding my pregnancy test purchase as I wrote my name on the counselor sign-in board. And there was Dev, marching past the main lodge, laughing, flanked on either side by his interchangeable Texan friends. Trent and Trevor were laughing for discernibly no good reason. They weren't even looking at one another as they laughed. But Dev didn't seem drunk at all. His eyes were crystalline blue. Then he took one look at Brian and me and suddenly his eyes weren't so clear

and blue anymore. Brian practically threw my pregnancy test at me.

"Where were you?" Dev asked. "You didn't show."

"The bouncer wouldn't let me in."

"Ro' got in. I saw her."

"I'm not Ro'. It's not my fault."

He eyed Brian curiously up and down, focusing on his spotless white sneakers.
"So you spent the night with Harvard Guy head of culture?"

Brian opened his mouth to say something but I quickly cut him off.

"His name is Brian," I corrected, as if we'd hung out all summer. Now I wished

we had. Brian drove a Prius. Brian listened to Bruce. Brian bought you pregnancy tests.

Dev wrinkled his nose, confused, like he hadn't seen this coming. He spotted

the plastic bag in my hand. "What's that?" he asked.

"What's this?" I dug my hand in and pulled out the pastel pink rectangular box

with the words PREGNANCY TEST in bold block letters. I wagged the box back and

forth in front of Dev's wild blue eyes. "It's a pregnancy test," I told him. "Can't you

read? Brian bought it for me while you were at the bar celebrating your birthday.

Pregnancy test. Preg. Nan.*Cy.*"

Brian just stood there, unsure of what to do. Trent and Trevor finally stopped

laughing. A few counselors gathered around us, a few of the Brits, some Swedes. DJ

Blake turned up and Elsa and Ingrid the Swedish twins. Everyone was looking at me. I

held the pregnancy test in my hand, above my head, like it was a grenade. Everybody waited. And then I did it. My big movie scene moment. I hurled the pregnancy test at Dev.

"Mushky!" he called after me.

But I was off, running and crying all the way back to my bunk. *Fuck*, I thought, tears streaming down my face, *Now the entire camp knows that I'm pregnant.*

—

I slipped quietly into bed. The last thing I wanted was to wake up my campers and have to pretend that everything was fine. They all lay asleep, breathing quietly in and out, curled up in their pretty pastel bedding. Even Margot looked angelic, snoring softly, her shiny black hair matted against her face.

Any minute Ro' would be back, dying to know what happened.

I didn't feel like talking. I rolled over onto my side, fetal position, tucking my hands beneath my pillow. I hated myself. I wanted to go home.

And like that, sleep took me.

—

I awoke early the next morning, hours before reveille, to an uncomfortable twinge in my stomach. A sliver of snowy-white moon lingered in the sky, a wan celestial smile hanging above camp. I watched it disinterestedly as a sharp cramp seized my abdomen. I felt nauseated, dizzy. My head was spinning. I pulled myself out of bed and made my way groggily toward the bathroom, pressing my right hand against the wall for balance. I locked the stall door and leaned over the toilet. This time I was sure: morning sickness.

I hadn't eaten in days so there wasn't much to heave. I fell to the floor with a dull thud and curled up in a ball, my knees pressed against my chest, my head against the toilet. I felt a heavy pressure in my bladder so I wriggled out of my pajama bottoms and slid down my underpants. And there it was.

My period.

I ran frantically to find Dev. I blew like a maniac into boys camp, as I'd done that first night in the rain when my cousin Shelli died, the night that started it all.

"Dev!" I called, flinging rocks at his bunk window. "Dev!"

He appeared so quickly on the bunk steps it was obvious that he hadn't been sleeping.

"Dev!" I cried. "I got my *period*!"

Dev hugged me tight. He swung me around. He dropped down to the ground on his hands and knees, raising his arms high into the air, his resounding yawp reverberating across camp: "G*ooooooooo* red team!"

6:00 P.M. Dinner

Miraculously, neither of us got fired. There was one week left of camp and I guess UG just didn't see the point. It wasn't worth the trouble of having to find two other counselors to take our place for the last few days and then actually have to pay them. Plus he'd already sacked a British kitchen boy for chucking his cigarette butt into the dumpster and igniting its contents into flames, and if you start firing too many people, the parents start to think there's something wrong with the camp and not the counselors.

The reality set in that my I might never see my campers again. And we were truly starting to like one another. I mean, really, really like one another. They followed me around camp like defenseless, unweaned puppies, tugging on my shorts and making me promise to come visit them in the fall. Samantha autographed her red bikini for me, scribbling her name with a pink Sharpie on the inside tag and circling it with a heart. "You can wear it when you come to stay with us in Palm Beach during winter vacation," she brightly suggested. "And I can wear your jeans."

Erika gave me the tiny jar with the snippet of Lindsay Lohan's pubic hair in it as a keepsake (It would someday be worth millions, she assured me. Maybe I could even sell it and use the money to pay for Yale). Ruth asked me to French braid her hair and thanked me for helping her through the whole period drama. "Every time I use a maxi pad I'll think of you," she told me, which oddly, didn't even really creep me out. She turned her big, round eyes up at me and asked, "When you get your period, will you think of me?" I told her that I would and I probably would because how can you not after someone asks you something like that?

Ashley/Ashland rolled up their posters of Zac Efron and Ashley Tisdale and gave them to me as gifts, hoping I'd tape them up on my dorm room walls when I went to college the following year. I was pretty sure if Yale ever accepted me they'd un-accept me if they saw those posters on my wall, but I told them that I would.

Even Margot sat on the edge of my bed during free period, quiet and contemplative as she listened to her iPod while I flipped through the required summer reading books that I never got around to actually reading.

And, of course, they sang to me:

> She's great, she's got spunk
> She's the counselor of our bunk
> Yea, Mushky! Yea, Mendelssohn!
> Yea, Yea! Mushky Mendelssohn!
> Mushky! Mendelssohn!
> Mushky Mendelssohn, Yea!

It was like my campers were all forgiving me in some way. Not that I'd been a bad counselor, but I had been a little remiss, fucking my boyfriend all summer on a mossy spot by the lake when I should have been focused on their crappy elective schedules or on what boys they'd developed crushes. I felt a pinch of guilt for having not been more there for them. There was so much I didn't know about my campers. I was shocked to hear that Ruth was a junior lifeguard, not until they handed out end-of-the-season Red Cross certificates during an evening ceremony on the waterfront.

Given the tremendous size of her boobs, I should have known they'd double as

flotation devises. And I had no idea that Erika had a boyfriend that she'd been seeing

for an entire four days and that his name was Adam Glass and that he lived in

Westport, Connecticut and played on a 12-and-under traveling soccer team and that

Erika "really, really, really, really, like *really*" liked him.

Erika's got a boyfriend! Erika's got a boyfriend!

Even Ro' grew wistful at the prospect of us not sharing a bunk, scribbling her

phone number on a book of matches with the Buckeye logo from the disastrous

Pregnancy Test Night.

"I can take the train from New York to Boston," she said, planning every little

detail of our post-camp friendship. "We can go shopping on Newbury Street and

spend the High Holidays together. We can take ski trips to Stowe and spend winter

break in South Beach at the Delano with the Kardashians. We can spend New Year's

Eve together and spring vacation and maybe do the Birthright Israel trip next summer.

And I can take you to this club I know in the city where Pete Wentz hit on me when I

was like fourteen and Ashlee Simpson was pregnant." She hopped ecstatically up and

down, clapping her hands like I'd won a nationwide Spelling Bee. "I'm just so glad that

you're not pregnant!"

I liked Ro,' I really did. But I was almost certain that I was never going to see

her supermodel posters again, and I was definitely certain that the story about Pete

Wentz was completely made up. Years later I might romanticize our friendship,

remembering it as something that it wasn't. But the truth was, our friendship was about two completely different people that wound up living together not out of any common interests, but out of shared circumstance. Put us in the same high school and I doubt we'd even acknowledge one another in the cafeteria. I wasn't sure we'd survive outside of camp, and anyway I had a friend a lot like her, too much like her, back home: Barrie.

That last week, Camp Kippewanscot yearbooks arrived, leather-bound with thick black spines, filled with summer highlights snapped by campers in the photography elective. For days, campers floated from bunk to bunk during rest hour with colored pens in hand, signing yearbooks in bubble-shaped cursive with cartoon hearts above the I's and drawing ☺ and XOXO beside their names and making idle promises to be BFFs and LOL and K.I.T.

Flipping through the yearbook, I identified myself in five pictures. Group bunk photo; a black-and-white still of me in the radio shack, my campers arranged in a circle on the floor listening to an iTunes shuffle; a snapshot of me and Ro' on the docks during a free swim, Ro' giving the peace sign because it matched her oversized Boho sunglasses and tie-dyed hair scarf; one of me in my red shirt during Color War; and then a shot of me during flag raising, arms stretched high above my head, my mouth agape in a yawn.

There wasn't a single picture in the Camp Kippewanscot yearbook of me and Dev together.

The night of the big final banquet, this whole big to-do where counselors and campers roasted one another and delivered mock prophesies for the future, the dining hall was decked out in garlands of party streamers and every table had confetti sprinkled all over it. It looked like the store Aaaaahs! had thrown up on it. Campers were encouraged to wear dressy attire, which for the girls meant skirts and dresses and headbands and for the boys meant clean underwear and laundered shorts. My campers predicted that Dev and I would wind up married and that I would head a popular radio station that played only Ashley Tisdale music. Everybody roared, even UG, if a bit contemptuously. Dev and I stood on opposite ends of the dining hall exchanging eye-rolls and wary glances. We were sick of all the songs and cheers and chants about us.

Sandwiched between the final banquet and the good-bye ice cream social by the lake was Tisha B'Av, the saddest day in the Jewish calendar. Campers had a choice between commemorating the destruction of the First and Second Temples or karaoke in the rec hall. Most chose karaoke. You're supposed to fast on Tisha B'Av because it's a really sad day, which was fine because I didn't have much of an appetite. I went to services hoping maybe Dev would show up in a yarmulke, maybe he'd come and atone for killing the chicken. But there were only three of us on the back porch of Darren's bunk: Me, Brian, who pretty much ignored me because he was scared that Dev would beat him up, and Hadar, the hippie Israeli dance teacher with hair under her armpits.

The fast ended and I phoned my parents.

"How was your fast?" I asked my mom.

"What fast?" she asked.

"The fast. It's Tisha B'Av."

"Not it's not," she said. "Tisha B'Av was last week."

Reform Jewish Camp Kippewanscot couldn't even get the date right.

Officially depressed, I wandered around camp looking for Dev. I found him in the computer shack downloading a bunch of files onto a disc.

"You're in a skirt," he said.

"It's a Jewish holiday," I told him. "Well, at least it was."

"Oh," is all he said, all fervor for my religion gone.

"Dev," I said. "What's going to happen when camp ends?"

"I'll go back to college."

"I mean, what's going to happen to *us*? What's really going to happen? Tell me. Whatever it is. I want you to tell me."

Dev ejected his disc from the computer and slid it into a protective sleeve.

"Come here," he said.

We sat on the floor with my head in his lap, and he ran his fingers through my hair like that first night at the welcome dance.

"I love you," he said.

"You do?"

"I do."

"You really do?"

"I do," he repeated, stroking my hair. "I love you. And I want us to be together. But for now, while I figure some things out in my head, right now, I need you to be..." He cleared his throat, "my *friend*."

Worst seven words ever spoken by a Gentile on the second to last day of summer camp.

7:30 P.M. Evening Activity

Last day of camp.

Campers and counselors congregated on the soccer field, awaiting busses to the airport and carpool rides home. A cool, end-of-summer breeze tickled the tips of the grass through which campers noisily clambered on a hunt for their parents. Everybody exchanged teary goodbyes, scrawled their addresses and telephone numbers on the backs of one another's hands and scraps of paper, making desperate, vain promises to write, call, email, IM, text, visit, Skype, Facebook, spend school vacations together, apply to the same private schools, request one another as bunk mates the following summer, go to the same college, live in the same neighborhoods when they grew up and send their kids to the same private schools.

> *We love you Kippewonscot*
> *Oh, yes we do!*
> *We'll miss you Kippewonscot*
> *And we'll be true*
> *When you're not with us, we're blue*
> *Camp Kippewanscot we'll always love you!*

Uncle Stan scooted along in his golf cart wearing a placid smile and waving at everybody. UG stalked around camp with his bullhorn, dictating orders and directing campers toward their respective places and screaming at everyone to "Move it! Move it! Move it!" like it was all part of an end-of-camp death march.

Most of my campers' parents all arrived on time. Ruth's mom thanked me for "helping to guide Ruth through her girlhood rite of passage," and pushed a hundred-dollar bill in my hand and a fresh sack of Floridian grapefruits. Ashley/Ashland's

mothers (even they looked alike) gave me a $100 gift certificate to iTunes and a $50

Barnes & Noble gift card. Margot's mother, witchy, raven-haired, with bags under her

eyes and a sharp stare, left no tip at all. But Margot gave me a desperate sort of hug,

like she never wanted to go home.

"You're sort of my favorite counselor," she whispered into my t-shirt.

"Wow. That's cool," I told her. "You're kind of my favorite camper."

She slid me a piece of paper with her email address on it:

DOOMSDAY1999@YAHOO.COM

Samantha and Mandy made a mad dash for the bus bound for Newark

International, disappearing from the soccer field without saying goodbye, unfazed by

the likelihood of never seeing me again or perhaps just excited to return home to their

nannies who made their beds and color-coded the clothes in their closets.

Ro' clomped toward the bus bound for New Rochelle, wearing the same stack-

heeled sandals she'd worn the first day of camp. When it came time to board, she

threw her arms around my neck and clung to me. "I'm so glad that we were co-

counselors," she told me. "There's something I've been wanting to tell you."

"What is it?"

"Did you ever wonder why I don't have a car?"

I shook my head. "No. I don't have one either."

"I know, but you're not rich like I am." She ripped open a fresh pack of

cigarettes and pulled one out for the ride. "I got a DUI," she said flatly. "My father pulled some strings so I don't have a record. But he took away my BMW for the summer. That's why I have to take the bus back to New Rochelle."

"That's no big deal, is it?"

"It is," she shrugged. "I could never admit that to any of my real friends from home. But you're different." She sighed. "Anyway, I'll have my BMW back by the time you come to visit me in a few weeks." She kissed me on the cheek, pivoted on her heels and climbed the stairs. She walked to the way back of the bus, plopped down in the last row, and kicked her long, lean legs up over the seat in front of her. She pushed down her window and lit up a cigarette. She blew smoke out the window and waved goodbye as the bus pulled away. Maybe I was wrong. Maybe I was going to miss her.

Heading back to the soccer field, I spotted Erika curled up under a tree by the goal post whimpering. "Your parents will be here soon," I told her, and sat down beside her on the grass. "They probably hit traffic."

"It's not my parents," she sobbed. "It's Adam, my boyfriend. After today I'll never see him again."

"Has he left yet?"

"He's over there." She pointed to the other side of the field where a group of twelve-year-old boys were tackling one another to the ground. The one in the beige shirt was Adam. "He's my first boyfriend," she cried. "We're getting married. Except suddenly he's acting like I don't even exist."

"Maybe he doesn't like goodbyes. Maybe he figures he's going to see you a lot after camp ends. He can come visit you, right?"

"No," Erika sniffled. "My mom doesn't let me have boys over. I already asked. She said not unless his mother stays over too, and his mother is married to some guy that's not his dad and they live in England or Alaska or somewhere cold like that."

"You can see him at the camp reunion in the winter."

Erika uttered a long lugubrious sigh, despondent in the wake of young love torn asunder. "That's easy for you to say," she said. "You're an adult. You're old. You get to see your boyfriend anytime you want."

I couldn't find Dev anywhere. The soccer field cleared out and I was the only counselor remaining. A flash of terror seized me. Had Dev left without saying goodbye? Then I remembered. I cut through the soccer field and walked to the main lodge where I found Dev in line with all the other staffers, waiting to collect our end-of-the-summer paychecks. Dev waved me over and, one by one, we entered the lodge, where envelopes with our checks inside were arranged alphabetically on a honey-colored table by last name: MCGILLICUDY, MENDELSSOHN. Together.

Linking hands, we walked to my bunk. It was the first time Dev had been inside all summer and somehow it all seemed symbolic. The walls were naked, stripped of posters and magazine tear-outs and pictures of Brazilian supermodels. The space was bare, spectral, like nobody had ever been in it. Next summer the walls would be plastered with new tween heartthrobs, the beds with new sheets, new sleeping bags, new blankets and pillows, new disturbing supermodel collages, new girls anxiously awaiting their periods, new counselors, new lives, new stories, new summer camp romances. I would be a memory, a ghost.

"I want to make love to you," said Dev. "Here. Right now."

He bent me over my bed and took me from behind. We did it with tears streaming down my face and my legs languidly parted as I regarded the view of the lake one last time through the open bunk window. When we were finished Dev said, "You're beautiful. So, so beautiful." After that, we didn't say much. We spooned on the hard narrow cot that I'd been sleeping in alone for the past eight weeks, the vinyl mattress cover crinkling as we shifted positions.

In a way, we wanted to get caught. And when UG walked by, opening the door to do a last-second check that all the campers were gone and had made their collective exodus home, when he saw us curled naked on the bed, flushed and sated, when he slammed the door behind him and ran right back out again, Dev and I laughed harder than we had all summer. We'd never come back here, never.

—

I dreaded every step to the parking lot. In moments I'd be boarding the staff bus to the airport, and Dev would be driving home to his mother.

We traversed the parking lot, staffers busily loading up their trunks with the vestigial stuff of summer: duffle bags, sleeping bags, beaded necklaces and hand-sewn moccasins from one of the art electives, nametags and counselor awards, pillows, blankets, sneakers and swimsuits, and contraband dime bags of weed they no longer cared about hiding.

The top to Dev's Camaro was already down. He popped the trunk, tossed his backpack inside and opened the door to the driver's side. I wanted him to open the passenger side and invite me to ride home with him, but of course he didn't. Instead, he reached inside the car and pulled out his ZBT baseball hat.

"I want you to have it," he said, pushing it down on my head and adjusting the back strap. The hat was warm and soft and smelled like Dev's sweaty head.

"This hat is holy to you," I told him.

"You've earned it," he said. "It's yours."

"So it's a goodbye gift," I said, looking down at the ground. "You mean this whole summer…and now all I get is a hat?"

"No," he told me, brushing his hand across my cheek. "Not goodbye. I'm going to see you soon. I'm going home to Syracuse to spend some time with my mother. I'll call you just as soon as I get back to Boston and get settled in my apartment. You'll know where I am. On Commonwealth Ave. We'll see each other all the time. I promise, Sunshine, I promise. The hat is just so you can feel me when we're apart."

Trent and Trevor came over and shook Dev's hand. "Good luck with everything, man." And then some of the Swedes crowded around us. They hadn't really spoken to anyone else but themselves all summer but now they kissed our cheeks and embraced us enthusiastically and invited us to their lake houses in Malmö. They waved and wished us "Adjö så lä´nge!" DJ Blake shouted out "Cheerio, mates!" realizing now how dumb it was pretending to be American all summer when his regular accent sounded so much cooler. Didn't he realize that Americans all wanted to be foreign?

Then Janice came up to me and placed her hand on my back the way she'd done when I wanted to slap her. "It was wonderful having you as a counselor," she told me. "So sorry again about your cousin." Brian Bluestein was standing beside his Prius. He looked over and gave me a little nod. Maybe I'd call him when I got back to Boston.

Maybe I was paranoid because of the whole pregnancy test episode, but it felt like everybody in the parking lot was staring at us, waiting for something to happen.

"I have to go now," said Dev.

"Right now?" I felt hot tears building up.

"Don't cry," he said, squeezing my shoulder. "We'll see each other soon."

"You promise?"

"I promise."

"OK," I sniffled. "I guess I should get on the bus."

"Fly safe," he said. "It's all going to be OK."

"Really?"

"Yes. Really."

"OK. Well, tell your mother I say hello."

He half-smiled, and swiped his sun-lit bangs to the side. He jingled his set of car keys, he way he'd jingled the set of keys from the Holiday Inn. He sighed in the direction of the car, then turned back around and grabbed my hand. "Oh, Mushky," he said. "I love you." Then he drew me close and kissed me hard.

In front of everyone.

9:30 P.M. Taps

Day is done
Gone the sun
From the Lakes
From the Hills
From the sky
All is well
Safely rest
God is nigh

Dev didn't call. He didn't visit.

I spent the first few weeks of my senior year of high school moping around the hallways in a fog, hoping that he would appear.

He never did.

Barrie kept asking me about it, kept asking about camp and if there were any cool girls that I met and whatever happened to that hot Jewish guy named Ron who wore a yarmulke outside of class? She'd come over after school and show me snapshots of her Thailand adventure and the sandals that she bought and all the colorful, pretty Thai dresses that she'd scooped up at some of the local shops along the Phuket beaches. She told me about running into Leonardo DiCaprio at a snorkel equipment rental stand and sitting next to Ewan McGregor at a café on the beach. She showered me with gifts: a pair of brown leather sandals, two dresses and a delicate gold bracelet with dangling heart charms she'd picked up on a day excursion to Bangkok. The tiny charms clinked every time I moved my wrists. Doing her part to edify the wrecked Tsunami-beaten coastline, Barrie went shopping whenever and wherever she could.

She had high hopes for her dad's new beachfront McDonald's: "You'll have to come with me next summer!"

She tried to get me to talk about my own summer, but I just couldn't.

Night after night I lay in bed unable to sleep. I'd stare at Dev's ZBT hat hanging limp on a hook on the back of my bedroom door, willing it magically to come to life. Occasionally, I'd take it down and wear it around the house. Once or twice my parents asked, "Did you meet a nice Jewish boy at camp?"

"No," I told them.

There was an evening in mid-September when my father was getting dressed for Rosh Hashanah services and I watched him in the full-length mirror adjusting his tie and came close to telling him what happened over the summer. But I didn't, because there wasn't much of a point. Bucky had had a blast at his gifted and talented summer science program at Johns Hopkins. He came back more gifted and more talented than before, padding around the house reciting algebraic equations and Einstein quotes.

I kept wondering how somebody that was once inside you could now seem so hopelessly far away. By now Dev had started first semester classes at Emerson. I looked for his Camaro on Commonwealth Ave, watched out for him on the T, tricked my mind into thinking I saw him at the Loews on Boston Common, convinced myself that he was standing in line at the Dunkin' Donuts on Tremont Street.

I called him on his cell phone, but the number was disconnected. I looked for him on Facebook. I found four other Devin McGillicudys—two in Boston, one in Chicago, one in Lincoln, Nebraska—but none of them were Dev.

Margot kept in touch. Her parents were going to finally let her go to Guatemala next summer to dig irrigation ditches and she was pretty excited about it. Erika wrote me a note saying that she and Adam had broken up—they hadn't so much as broken up as he never wrote to her in the first place—but that she was seeing someone new from the next town over and that he played baseball and not soccer and that was way cooler anyway.

It was nice to hear from them, but they weren't Dev. And the dozens of postcards and letters that I fielded from campers, all the pastel envelopes affixed with rainbow stickers and unicorn address labels, made the rejection sting even more.

It didn't matter if all the signs were there, or that I maybe half-imagined how much he loved me, or that he'd been telling me all along that he wasn't going to be there for me. It still didn't take away the fact that out of camp, with nothing between us except four T-stops and a three-mile stretch of Commonwealth Avenue, Dev was farther away now than he was all summer in Kelev unit in boys camp.

You're an adult. You get to see your boyfriend anytime you want.

A month passed. Then two.

One day, I couldn't take it anymore. I ran madly up and down Commonwealth, searching for the name MCGILLICUDY on every buzzer door. I never found it. I surfed the Emerson College website, where I found alumni news about Jay Leno and the guy that co-created *Friends*, but nothing about Dev. I went for long walks around the

Emerson campus, hoping for a glimpse. My parents were not very pleased, not

because they knew that I was loitering around a college campus looking for a boy, but

because it was the wrong type of college.

"I thought you wanted to go to Yale," my mother said to me. "Why are you

suddenly so interested in Emerson?"

"If you're going to take out tens of thousands of dollars in student loans to go to

Emerson, than you might as well take all that money and go to Yale so you can get a

job where you make enough money to pay back the loans that you took out," said my

dad.

In early November I mustered up the guts to sign up for a prospective student

tour, pretending to be interested in Emerson's BFA program so that I could roam

through its buildings—you needed a VISITOR badge—where I was sure that I would

find Dev.

I wore a snug grey wool sweater and one of my mother's black Cashmere

scarves from the 1980's. I wore skinny jeans that I tucked into a pair of suede, knee-

high boots that Barrie let me borrow. I kept my hair loose (I put tons and tons of

conditioner in it) and toted a brown leather messenger bag. I looked pretty,

sophisticated, collegiate.

And there, wandering off from a tour of a ceramics class that I never planned to

attend, thinking of pinch pots and palettes and MUSHKY and DEV engraved on the

back, standing in the middle of the Arts Quad, I found him.

There he was.

Kissing a girl. Her. Not-So-Original Jennifer. The one he'd obviously been calling all summer.

I wanted to run, but I also wanted to stab him in the chest until his heart split open into a thousand little pieces.

"Mushky?" he said. He squinted under his fair yellow bangs that he'd cut since last time I'd seen him. "Mushky?"

He whispered something into Jennifer's ear then made some sort of motioning gesture for her to stay put. He took a deep breath and walked toward me.

"Mushky." He faltered. "Mushky." I hated the way he said my name. "Mushky, what are you doing here?"

"I'm taking a tour of the campus."

"You want to go to Emerson?"

"No," I flatly responded. "I'm way too smart for Emerson. Is that Jennifer?" I asked, even though I knew it was.

I nodded at Jennifer. She coolly smiled. She had long, straight, perfect, snag-free hair through which Dev could most certainly run his fingers with no conditioner and no trouble at all. She dug her hands into her blazer pockets and shifted around on her college girl clogs, pretending to not pay attention to us.

"Mushky—"

"Stop it," I snapped. "Stop saying my name."

"I'm sorry."

"Sorry about what?

"I'm sorry that things just didn't work out."

"You never called me," I said. "You never emailed. You pretended that I'd never even existed."

"That's not true, Mushky."

"You told me you loved me. You told me that we'd see one another all the time."

"I know I did—"

"So what? So you just forgot? You just moved back to Boston, started school and got back together with Jennifer?"

"Mushky—"

"Did I not just ask you to *stop* saying my name?"

Jennifer rubbed her hands together and blew on them. It was getting cold outside, fall's first snappy chill.

"Did you even break up with her?" I asked. "Were you with her that whole entire time?"

Dev sighed. "Look," he said. "I tried to explain—"

"Explain what?"

"We both knew it could never work out."

"Explain *what*?"

"I wanted to tell you—"

"When? When we were having sex? When you were telling me that you loved me? When I thought that I might be pregnant—"

"I was confused."

"Tell me *what*?"

"Mushky, this is hard for me—"

"You said she wasn't original. You said you didn't feel that *thing* for her. Remember, when you tried to convince me to be with you? You lied to me. You lied to me all summer. You deleted her from your iPhone but you didn't delete her from your life."

"We're the same age, Mush— " He caught himself. "We're both seniors in college. We're both going through the same thing."

"You told me that age didn't matter. Remember? When you pursued me? You told me that age didn't matter and that religion didn't matter and that nothing mattered except you and me. But it was all a bunch of crap, wasn't it?"

"Mushky, come on, you never really loved me."

"You lied to me. All summer long. You fucking lied to me."

"No. You don't understand. It's not like that at all."

"And all those calls from your…*mother*? Bullshit. It was all a bunch of bullshit."

"Listen to—"

"You made a complete fool out of me. You made me look like an idiot. You used me, Dev. You used me. I hate you. I hate you. I *hate* you…"

And I stood there in the middle of the Arts Squad, sobbing hysterically as a procession of students in pea coats and J. Crew sweaters and navy blazers all looked on, all the while Dev and Jennifer exchanging awkward glances, neither sure what to do. I despised myself for letting them see me this way. I despised myself for having loved him.

"Why?" I asked him. "Why? Just tell me *why?*"

But Dev didn't say a word.

And that about said everything.

—

Berkowitz believed he had the answer: "He's a jerk and he's a goy."

But I knew that it wasn't that simple. Dev could have been anything – Catholic, Muslim, Hindu, atheist, or a Druze like the guy Lizzie Applebaum married. Dev could have been Jewish. Things might have turned out pretty much the exact same way.

Finally, I went to see a shrink. I didn't have anyone else that I wanted to talk to and it seemed like an easy enough solution. Plus, everyone went. Barrie's mother was always going and my parents' friends and all their kids, including Aaron Epstein now that he was going to be history's first Jewish teenage father (not really, but that's what his mother kept running around weeping about to everyone in a panic). And now my brother Bucky was in therapy because at some point during his gifted and talented summer science program at Johns Hopkins he got a nose ring and decided that because he was so gifted and talented high school was a colossal waste of time, and that he was going to drop out and move to Butte, Montana with his dorm mate and grow organic vegetables and become a glass blower.

The shrink's office was grey and had posters of plants all over its walls, but no actual plants. There was a wooden coffee table with copies of *Time* and *Self*, and a little round alarm clock with a glow-in-the-dark face that lit up green whenever the sun disappeared behind the tree outside the window and a grey shadow was cast across the room. The shrink wore grey wool slacks and a turtleneck sweater and I kept picturing Dev's turtleneck penis. Her hair was pulled back in a bun wound so tight it gave her a mini-facelift.

"Were you in love with Dev?" the shrink asked me that first session.

I told her about how we met and how he wore his ZBT baseball hat to impress me, and how he'd come to Shabbat services and called me "Sunshine" for a while and talked about converting and how we named our unborn children and about my cousin dying and that first night on the grass by the lake late at night and how I thought that I was pregnant.

"But were you in *love* with him?"

It was the middle of November. Outside of the office window, the leaves were falling in shades of red, orange and gold. They'd made a crunching sound under my boots as I stepped over them on my way from the Pleasant Street T stop to the shrink's red brick Coolidge Corner office building. It was like a million years had passed since summer.

"I'm not sure," I answered. "It felt good, at first. And then it felt bad. And that part lasted much longer."

"Why did it feel good?"

"I don't know," I shrugged. "He pursued me. He convinced me that we should be together. And suddenly all the reasons that we shouldn't be together made it all seem so...."

"Romantic."

"*Alive*," I told her. "I felt things that I'd never before felt. I felt everything. Sickening. Shameful. Desperate. Sad. Lonely. Happy. Confused. Dev made me feel alive."

"And what happened?"

"He pulled away," I told her. "And everything changed. And the good part didn't even last that long. But I held onto it, because I wanted to. And when he lied to me, when he did things that I should have questioned, when he told me who he really was..." I thought about that very first night together on the mossy bank of the lake. "I guess I just wanted to believe that when good things happen they stay that way forever."

"And is that being in love?" she asked.

I stared around the office at the posters of plants that weren't really plants and ran my hand across the sofa's warm velour fabric.

"No," I answered. "I guess it's not."

—

Eventually, it all made sense. Or at least as much sense as it ever would.

Dev had told me things I wanted to believe and I believed them because I wanted to. And when he told me these things weren't true, I still believed him. Because I wanted to be in love. Because I wanted to have that experience. Because, in my own way, I wanted to be in love with someone with whom it could never work. It was like Dev said, the one thing he actually got right about me: at seventeen, I really was too young to worry about it working out for the long run with anyone.

December was filled with the SATs, and college admissions essays, and getting drunk for the first time at a high school football game keg party with Barrie, an "A" on an essay that I wrote for my AP English class on George Eliot's *Middlemarch* (I finally read it), clothes shopping for a blazer to wear to college interviews, and an airplane ticket in the mail from Berkowitz to visit him in California for two weeks over winter break. I even ran into Brian Bluestein one Sunday in Harvard Square where I'd gone to pick Berkowitz out a Chanukah gift. We chatted for a bit, but he was with a girl who wore clean white sneakers just like his, and I was a little jealous, but I could see that they were perfect for one another.

I wasn't completely happy, but I wasn't completely *not* happy. I wasn't so worried anymore about what was going to happen in the future, or if Yale was going to accept me or what sort of job I'd get when I got out. For what seemed like the first time in my entire teenage life, I just...*was*. I listened to the music I liked, and spent time with my friends when I liked, and did pretty much what teenagers do and had fun with it all as much as I could.

And every once in a while, I'd flip through the pages of the Camp Kippewanscot yearbook. I'd look at all the pictures of me and Ro' and Margot and Erika and Ashley/Ashland and Samantha and Ruth, and miss everybody from that summer like mad.

There were moments when I wanted to call Dev and tell him about all of it.

But I knew that I couldn't.

So I picked up the phone and called Berkowitz.

Somewhere up in heaven, my Russian-Jewish great-grandmother was beaming.

10:00 P.M. Lights Out

CPSIA information can be obtained at www.ICGtesting.com
Printed in the USA
LVOW051337150313

324495LV00004B/58/P